PRAISE FOR *DO*

M000164769

"Claustrophobic and suffocating twist of this edge-of-your-seat winter thriller will chill you to the bone. Parrack spins a tale of survival and found family that will [in] equal parts delight and terrify you. I couldn't stop reading—safely under my covers."

—Rebecca Hanover, *New York Times*
bestselling author of *The Similars*

"The action is fast-paced, with just enough romantic tension... [a] comfortingly familiar page-turning suspense."

—*Kirkus Reviews*

"[For] readers who like mysteries that defy imagination."

—*Youth Services Book Review*

"I shivered my way through this survival tale, in which no place is safe for long, and no one can be trusted."

—Parker Peevyhouse, author of *The Echo Room*

"A tense thriller that tightens the screws on every page. A worthy addition to the genre!"

—Gretchen McNeil, author of *Ten* and *#murdertrending*

"Parrack's latest brings nonstop action... Readers will appreciate Lottie's emotional journey in the wake of so many disappointments in her life, all while being tested in unfamiliar circumstances, from both nature and humankind."

—*Booklist*

ALSO BY KEELY PARRACK

Don't Let in the Cold

10
HOURS
TO GO

10 HOURS TO GO

KEELY PARRACK

sourcebooks
fire

Copyright © 2024 by Keely Parrack
Cover and internal design © 2024 by Sourcebooks
Cover design by Erin Fitzsimmons/Sourcebooks
Cover photos © Aaron Davis/EyeEm/GettyImages, plainpicture/harry +
lidy, Anan Kaewkhammul/Shutterstock, Leo Fernandes/Shutterstock
Internal design by Laura Boren/Sourcebooks

Sourcebooks and the colophon are registered trademarks of Sourcebooks.

All rights reserved. No part of this book may be reproduced in any form or by
any electronic or mechanical means, including information storage and retrieval
systems—except in the case of brief quotations embodied in critical articles or
reviews—without permission in writing from its publisher, Sourcebooks.

The characters and events portrayed in this book are fictitious or
are used fictitiously. Any similarity to real persons, living or dead,
is purely coincidental and not intended by the author.

Published by Sourcebooks Fire, an imprint of Sourcebooks
P.O. Box 4410, Naperville, Illinois 60567–4410
(630) 961-3900
sourcebooks.com

Cataloging-in-Publication Data is on file with the Library of Congress

Printed and bound in the United States of America.
VP 10 9 8 7 6 5 4 3 2 1

To Adam and Luka, for all the roads taken, and those yet to come.

AFTERNOON

Friday, September 6

1

A BELL TOWER CHIMED, THREE O'CLOCK. NATASHA WAS late. I should have predicted it.

I bet she hadn't changed since middle school. But twenty minutes added on to a ten-hour drive wouldn't make much difference, and she was coming from across town. I checked the Portland traffic on my phone. Totally clear. She probably hadn't even left yet.

I sat on the stone steps outside the lecture hall, hugging my knees, watching as one by one, everyone on my Oak Canyon College tour got picked up and swept away. The confident ones by Ubers, the rich ones by taxis, and the last few by parents—anxious to help their kids make the best college choice in this step to adulting. I know, who was I to judge? Still, it passed the time.

The hazy sun shimmered through the leaves of a gnarled beech tree and settled on the white patches of skin visible through the holes in my black jeans. I refolded my hoodie to make a softer cushion against the hard bench.

This whole place was a fantasy college—Gothic redbrick buildings complete with gargoyles, arched walkways, quiet courtyards, shady tree-lined pathways, and a huge meadow dotted with heritage trees and laughing students. This time next year it could be me laughing with my friends, strolling to my next class, or studying in the oak-beamed library. The possibility lit a fire in my heart. This was my dream, and I was going to make it happen.

I smiled to myself. A blue-haired student passing by smiled back. Everyone was so friendly. Mom was right. There was nothing like seeing the place for real to know if it was a good fit or not. I didn't even need to see anywhere else. My heart was set.

All that stood in the way was Mom's test results, and she'd been feeling so well lately they were likely to be good. Mom would be so happy I'd found the right place. I pulled out my phone and texted.

Love it here!!!! Can't wait to tell you all about it.

It was totally worth the long train ride up. At least going back, I wouldn't have to deal with the train constantly stalling. It was fire season; one whiff of smoke and everything got delayed and now my return trip had been canceled. Thank God I'd found a ride.

I stood and stretched like I was completely fine waiting alone. A student ran by with her little corgi dog, both dressed in burgundy sweatshirts with the college logo of a little owl on the front.

Then finally, half an hour late, Natasha arrived.

She waved from her shiny gray Prius, and called out, "Hey, Lily!" like we were old friends, like nothing had ever happened between us. I smiled back and climbed in.

Natasha was effortlessly polished, just as I remembered her. Her dark-brown hair was long and glossy and her eyebrows perfectly arched. Her light tanned skin was flawless. Even her freckles were perfectly placed across her sun-kissed nose.

She eyed my hair. "Wow, love the highlights! Red, huh? That's a bit bold for the Lily I knew, isn't it?"

"I guess I'm not that Lily anymore." I fake smiled back, attached my seat belt, and ran my hand through my shoulder-length brown hair, red streaks and all.

"Here, I got you a sparkling water for the ride." Natasha pointed to the can of sparkling cherry water in the cupholder.

"Oh thanks." Kindness was not what I'd been expecting.

"That smoky haze is something else, isn't it?" She glanced out the window. "Hope we're not driving toward it."

"It doesn't look too bad. At least there've been fewer fires than normal this year."

"True that," said Natasha as she looked down at my patchwork messenger bag "Is that your only bag?"

"Yep. It was an up-one-day, back-the-next kind of deal." I shoved my bag down by my feet. "I guess I could have waited up here an extra day, but... Thanks so much for picking me up last minute and everything." I said it all in a rush, like I was nervous. Which I totally was not.

"Yes, I heard that a fire crossed the tracks. When my mom called, I was surprised. But it's no problem. I didn't realize our moms still talk to each other. Luckily for you, or you'd be stranded, I guess." She paused to watch a guy and his dog cross the street. A student probably—they even let you keep pets here. "I can't believe you came all this way to visit one school."

3

Put like that, it sounded totally ridiculous. "It's the only one I'm interested in up here." Two minutes in, and I was already justifying myself. Maybe she wasn't trying to catch me out; maybe she was just being curious. "It's such a great school."

"It's good to know your own mind." Natasha tapped her cherry-tipped nails on the steering wheel. "Ready?" She didn't wait for a reply before silently pulling away, leaving Oak Canyon College behind us.

As she drove, I tried and failed to think of something interesting to say and ended up with, "How were your college visits?"

"Oh, I'm not going to college up here. Just visiting friends. A friend. Things kind of unraveled, so I'm headed back early." She paused for a moment with her lips pursed. "So how was your visit? Let me guess." She frowned as if she was considering. "Small, private, green, lacking the token diversity depicted on their website? Your usual liberal arts deal." She tilted her chin as if daring me to disagree. "You'll be fine, Lily. I bet they loved you." She almost sounded sincere.

"It's actually pretty diverse, and yes, I will be fine." My cheeks ached from fake smiling. I *would* get in, and I didn't need her assurance. This was so surreal. I felt like I was twelve again, justifying myself to Natasha. I looked for signs of anything: anger, hate, pity, but she was focused on the road. It was so long since we'd spent any time together, so it's not like either of us knew each other now. Was she going to say anything about what happened back then, or was the past a closed book? If she was ignoring it, I was happy to play along.

Natasha glanced at me. "I didn't think Oak Canyon was your vibe. I would have thought it was a bit too intellectual, too quirky. Though I guess people can change." Her copper eyes sparkled. I knew that look. She was baiting me already. How did I ever think this ride was a good idea?

She carried on. "I mean you might enjoy Portland. It's just so small and rainy. Well, normally. I guess not this year."

A truck honked as we merged a little too slowly onto the Ross Island Bridge Road.

"I like the small-city, anything-goes vibe."

"Keep Portland weird!" Natasha laughed. "You'd fit in there then. You've always been a little off-kilter."

WTF? I took a deep breath. "Yes, it's fun to try somewhere a little different from where you come from, I think." The green-gray river slipped by beneath us. This place was all bridges and weed stores. "Nice to leave California and experience something different."

"I guess," Natasha said like she didn't think so at all.

"There's no guarantee I'll get in anyway." Why did I say that?

"Tell me about it. What's your GPA, again?" She cut across two lanes, narrowly avoiding scraping up against an SUV.

"Pretty good." High enough to dream. I gripped my seat as we slid back into the right lane. "I'm counting on my SATs to help."

"You know they don't really use them anymore. It's all on your GPA, unless you write an amazing essay on overcoming trauma." Natasha always did love to needle me. She took a sharp left, everything in the car rolled to the side. "Maybe you can lean on your mom's story for that."

Oh. My. God. She was really going there. "She's doing much better now." I glared out the window. My first instincts were right. Natasha had not changed at all.

"Oh, great," Natasha said, as if breast cancer was a headache my mom had gotten over.

And this was why I never should have listened to my stupid mother. So what if Amtrak was delayed from fires and wasn't running past Eugene today? So what if the replacement bus bridge running from Eugene to Oakland added an extra six hours? A twenty-hour trip home alone would have been easier than knowing I had ten hours to go, trapped in a car with Natasha.

After all this time, I'd forgotten how she made me feel. There was a reason I'd avoided her in high school. I'd outgrown her, moved on. My skin crawled at the thought of small talk all the way home. Playing nice. Pretending everything was fine. Maybe I could just fake sleep instead—yeah, right, for six hundred miles.

"So, what's your college plan?" I asked her. Anything to avoid talking about me.

"I'm joining my sister at Stanford, with UC Berkeley as my B plan."

I shook my head. "You haven't changed. Only you would have Berkeley as plan B."

"Everyone needs a backup plan." She scowled in the rearview mirror at the truck behind us. It actually slowed down and stopped tailgating. "Do you know my dad almost went to Oak Canyon, but he changed his mind? Too far from home, too small, too insular." She grinned, like I wouldn't know she was really talking about me.

"Too bad." I checked my phone. Mom hadn't texted back.

"Hope you don't still get carsick." Natasha glanced at me. "Do you remember when my mom drove us to Monterey, and we had to stop like twelve times so you wouldn't puke in our new car?"

"Nope." Thanks for reminding me. "Maybe keep your eyes on the road?" Jesus, we'd be dead before dark at this rate.

"I forgot what a worrier you are about everything." She stared at me mouth open, then slammed the brakes just in time to miss the white Chevy truck in front of us. "Seriously, a slowdown already?"

"I guess we should have planned for it. It is fire season." I checked the map app on my phone. "I'll plug in our route. There's a delay coming up. An hour." Eleven hours to San Ramon. Eleven long hours home. "Do you want to share the driving?"

"God, no. It's the only thing that will keep me from being bored to death!"

I honestly couldn't tell if she meant from me or from the road trip. Or maybe she just didn't realize how rude she sounded.

"Oh God, sorry." She giggled. "That came out sooooo wrong! I didn't mean bored of you. I'm dying to catch up." Again, sarcasm or truth? I couldn't tell. But I let it go and gave a quick reassuring smile.

She turned up the radio.

Smoke still drifting north, as far as Multnomah County from the Wolf Hollow fire, which is also causing slowdowns on the I-5 South from the Cottage Grove exit. No road closures yet. And sadly, no chance of that rain we're all praying for but a chance of thunderstorms rolling in this evening with possible dry lightning. And with that, the threat of more wildfires. Stay safe out there, people.

"Dry lightning? Remember all those fires that started last time?" Natasha asked.

"That was the worst. So strange to get all that lightning and no rain." I used to love thunderstorms, but not anymore. "We'll be well out of Oregon by then, right?" I asked.

"For sure." Natasha blew a stray hair from her eyes. "We just have one more stop, and then it's five hundred miles down this boring freeway home."

I stared at her. "One more stop?" This was going to take forever.

"Did you think your rideshare was just for one? Anyway, you know her."

"Who is it?" My gut warned me this was not good news.

"Elke. Remember Elke? We're picking her up from Eugene." And Natasha hummed along to the radio again, like picking up Elke was nothing.

I sat in stunned silence. *Elke.* I bit my lip. Elke whose life I'd ruined in eighth grade, *that* Elke? I finally stuttered, "Elke Azizi?" As if it could possibly be anyone else.

"Yes." Natasha smiled, like it was a good thing. "It's going to be so much fun." I couldn't tell if she meant that to sound sarcastic.

Perhaps Elke wouldn't remember me. Like she wouldn't remember that I'd got her expelled. That I'd never got to face her and say sorry. Not that it mattered. The past was past. I sat up straighter and smoothed my hair. "I think I do remember her, vaguely," I added. And smiled like nothing was wrong. Because it wasn't.

Natasha had made sure that my version of the truth never fully came out. As if I'd been the one who ruined Yosemite Adventure

Camp. It was all their fault. They'd organized the secret midnight party. It was lucky I was there to yell *Fire!* when their campfire got out of control. I was trying to do a good thing when I'd told on Elke. Trying to protect people. Instead, Natasha shamed me for snitching on my friends. Just remembering the hallway whispers, the rumors, and side-eyes made me shiver. How was I supposed to know Elke would get into so much trouble?

And now Elke was going to be here in the car, and there was no escape.

I bet Natasha and Elke were still besties. It would be two against one. I would have to pretend nothing was wrong all the way home.

It wasn't like I was going to ever see them after the ride. But my stomach rolled because I knew there was no getting around it. This was going to be the road trip from hell.

2

I DIDN'T RECOGNIZE ELKE AT FIRST. I WAS LOOKING FOR A girl with light-brown skin and long blond hair dressed in some sort of flowery minidress. Right, because everyone always wore their outfits from middle school for the rest of their life. Perhaps she imagined me in the hand-me-downs my mom used to make me wear to school. Thank God, those days were over.

This long-legged girl stood with her back to me, nonchalantly leaning against the bus stop. She shook her bob-cut violet hair and slid her phone into the back pocket of her shorts. Her chunky rose-embroidered Doc Martens made sure she stood out from the crowd of milling students like a lemur at a petting zoo. Not dangerous, but definitely not ordinary. She turned and beamed at Natasha, and I knew immediately it was her. Four years after everything, I was finally facing Elke again.

My heart beat double time. Did she hate me? I held my breath preparing for the worst.

She came bounding over. "Thanks so much, Nat. You're a lifesaver. I so appreciate this!" She glanced at me and frowned. "Lily, isn't it, from middle school?" Natasha must have warned her already. "You look so different!"

"I am so different." I said, tilting my chin like the confident person I was now.

"I'm Elke, by the way. In case you've forgotten me."

"Hi." I gave a little wave. OMG, why did I do that?

Elke opened my door. "I need to be up front. I get horrendous car sickness!" She was actually expecting me to jump out for her.

I put on my best fake smile and squirmed in my seat. "I get carsick, too."

"Not as bad as her," Natasha cut in. "Go on, Lily. There's more room in the back. You can lie down if you need to." She gave me a nod, as if I'd said yes already. "Thanks."

"Yes, thanks, Lily," Elke added, moving aside for me to exit.

I sighed, gathered my bag, and got out. I climbed into the back seat and rearranged myself there.

"God, it's so dry and smoky out there." Elke pushed her seat back, giving me an inch of leg room. "Ugghhhh, can't wait for fire season to be over."

I crossed and uncrossed my legs, trying to figure out where to put my knees.

"Oh, there's a water here for you." Natasha pointed to the unopened can of sparkling cherry water she'd given to me earlier. "There's one in the back for you, Lily."

"Thanks," I said, spotting it rolling on the floor. Great. I put it in the cupholder, hoping it wouldn't make a giant fizzy mess by the time I opened it.

Elke searched inside her backpack and pulled out a CD. "I made a road-trip mix that we can play later."

She obviously knew Natasha's Prius was so old it had a CD player. They must have stayed in touch. Of course, they did. When Elke was forced to leave the school, it probably only made their friendship stronger.

Natasha put the car in gear. "Ready?"

"Let's go! Road trip!" Elke danced in place, bouncing her seat against my legs. "Oops, sorry," she said before I could get annoyed. "I didn't realize we were that close," she added and pulled her seat forward an inch. "Better?"

I nodded. And it was.

Just thinking about middle school made my palms sweat. But Elke chatted away like nothing was wrong. The places she'd been to for sushi, how bad the traffic was, how the party was last night (*wild*). By the time we'd glided out of the University of Oregon, back onto the main road, I had relaxed. It was just a ride. Everything was going to be fine.

Stay on the I-5 South for 438 miles, Natasha's map app directed us. Smooth sailing. Finally, I could just slip away and pretend I wasn't there. It wasn't like they minded. Too busy catching up on their summer vacations to Amsterdam (Elke) and Florence (Natasha).

"What about you, Lily, go anywhere fun?" Elke was not going to let me disappear after all.

I gave a half laugh. "This was it, day trip to Portland." First time I'd been away in two years. "My mom's been sick, so I don't get out much."

"Oh." Elke tapped at her phone. "Sasha is texting me, like I need to be checked up on." She rolled her eyes at Natasha. Then turned back to me. "Sorry, what was that about your mom?"

"Nothing." I took out my phone, just to look busy and see if Mom had texted back. Nope, which was strange for her. She probably didn't want to annoy me by texting me too much. But no news was good news. "So, umm, were you on a college tour?"

"What?" Elke sounded like she'd forgotten I was even in the car behind her. "Oh yeah. No, I was helping Sasha, my ex, move into her dorm. I don't think I'm cut out for college. Too much, you know, work." She grinned at Natasha. "And no parental expectations, so..." Her eyes drifted off to the passing scenery.

We drove along the slow-moving freeway, caught in between trucks and RVs, passing meadows, the occasional trailer park, and farm supply stores. We even passed by a shirtless guy, all ribs and stretched-out pale skin, riding his bike along the shoulder. Eventually the freeway became a winding road heading into the forest-covered mountains. Only the closest trees were visible; the rest of the landscape was behind a hazy smog. And the traffic was getting worse.

"Welcome to late summer in Oregon!" Elke said. "Jeez, fire season gets worse every year."

"Wait." I frowned. "I thought you moved to DC or somewhere?" Somewhere far enough away for us to never see each other again.

"Hah, I didn't realize you were keeping tabs on me. I did move to DC, but now I'm back in San Ramon." She smiled at me. "Got a problem with that?"

I shook my head. Nope. This trip was getting better and better.

We slowed down to ten miles an hour, then five. The traffic crept along, bumper to bumper, until it disappeared into the smoky haze ahead.

"Is this from the Wolf Hollow fire? I didn't realize it was that close." Elke pulled out her phone. "We should use my TRX app, it's better."

"Maybe there's an accident ahead?" I suggested.

"Yes," said Elke, "or maybe a *fire*." She said it like I was an idiot.

I glared at the back of her violet head.

"We have to stay on I-5 South for miles unless there's a detour around this slowdown." Natasha gave Elke a little nod, like she was trying to tell her something. Or maybe I was reading in things that weren't there.

"Look." Elke thrust her phone in Natasha's face. "We're going to be crawling soon. There's a two-hour delay."

"One hour." I cleared my throat. "The radio said one hour earlier."

"Yes, *earlier*—like when you were back in Eugene. Now we're looking at two hours." Elke cracked open her can of water, sucking the top as it spilled over the edge.

The last thing we needed was to get off course. "It will probably flow again any minute. It could just be rubberneckers, looking at a road accident or the remnants of one. It's probably been moved to the side already," I said hopefully.

"TRX says there's a fire. Looks like it's spreading closer to the freeway." Elke raised her chin, daring me to disagree. "It's still, like, ten miles away."

"That's not far," I said. "I bet it speeds up after that."

Natasha slammed on the brakes. The traffic stopped suddenly as if everyone had been plugging into their map apps at the same time and had only just looked up at the road.

I caught Natasha discreetly raising her brows at Elke.

"Okay, what's the next exit?" Elke looked around at me like I'd know.

I shrugged and looked out just in time to catch the digital traffic sign.

RED FLAG WARNING, EXTREME FIRE DANGER AHEAD

Well, duh. I checked my text messages, still nothing from Mom. No news was good news. I murmured that like a mantra.

"Hey, we're close to Dope Donuts. I've been dying to go there. Sasha says it's amazing. It's only twenty minutes away, and I bet we can find a route from there that skips this backup." Elke clapped her hands with excitement.

Natasha's face lit up. "Sounds great! What do you think, Lily?"

"Dope Donuts?" Nope.

Elke flashed a grin at me and pointed at the upcoming exit sign. "We'll get off at that exit, and back on three exits later." She tapped out a message on her phone. "Just letting Darius know we're hitting his favorite place."

"Is that okay with you, Lily?" Natasha caught my eyes in the mirror.

"Who's Darius?" The name sounded vaguely familiar.

"Oh, just Sasha's brother." Elke glanced at Natasha. They both tried not to smile.

Whatever. "I have to get back." For Mom's test results. But they didn't need to know that.

"Like a half-hour detour?" Elke raised her brows. "It'll probably save us time, instead of sitting here going nowhere for two hours."

"I don't know." It's not like I could say no without being a killjoy. "Look, the drive's already so long." I tried to sound reasonable.

Two-hour traffic delay ahead. But still the fastest route to our destination.

Elke turned around and stared at me intently, daring me to refuse.

I sighed and looked at Natasha in the mirror. She shrugged. "It's an extra hour, tops. You owe her that much."

My stomach dropped. There it was. Natasha smiled at me as if she'd said nothing. Heat rushed to my cheeks. What could I say? It felt like I was in eighth grade with them both all over again, feeling small and friendless. Shit. That was not me. That was not who I was now. I swallowed hard, too flustered to get my words out.

Elke smiled. "Is that a yes?" She pouted like it was all a joke. "Pretty please?"

I nodded. "Okay, yes, fine."

"Great!" Elke practically bounced in her seat. "Let me just check those directions," she said looking at her phone. "The exit is one mile ahead and then we'll take a right." She rummaged in her bag. "Gum, anyone?"

It was strange how all the tension in the car vanished as soon as I'd said yes. Like that was it, and the past was totally forgotten. But my gut churned with all those old memories. I pushed them down, determined to only show the new me, the fun, totally normal, confident me.

"Would you rather be a rhino or a hippo?" Elke asked.

I thought she was joking until she frowned at me. "Come on, rhino or hippo?"

I glanced at Natasha but she seemed to think it was no big deal.

"Hippo," I finally decided, "because they're amazing swimmers and also deadly."

"Hah, nice answer," said Elke. "Natasha, what about you?"

"Rhino, so I can charge at you with my horn when you make people play car games."

"Fair enough. Oh, there's the exit." Elke pointed at it.

3

WE TURNED OFF, BYPASSING A GIFT STORE WITH GIANT
red-and-white papier-mâché mushrooms balanced on its roof, even
though Elke really wanted to go in, and followed a winding road
past a golf course edged with brambles and pine trees, past fields
with rows of rusted tractors and plastic-covered hay bales, and a
dust devil twisting in a dried-up field.

"There it is!" Elke swung her head as we sped by it.

Natasha pulled a quick U-turn. A mud-splattered white pickup
truck blared its horn as Natasha cut in front of it.

The store was nestled between a diner and a gas station. It seemed
like everyone had the same idea as we did to get off the highway.
People milled outside Mike's Diner, staring at the girls who'd almost
caused a crash.

"Forget about that. Let's get those doughnuts!" Elke said.

Natasha looked up at the store sign. "Bud-Bliss? Really?" She
rolled her eyes, but Elke grabbed her hand and pulled her along. I
trailed behind.

Inside the store, glass cabinets lined the walls full of samples, rainbow gummies, gooey brownies, glowing candies, pipes, and bongs. The shelves behind the counter were full of glass storage jars piled high with dried-green weed buds. Turns out Dope Donuts was not the name of the store, but one of the many products sold at Bud-Bliss. Fortunately, the dope doughnuts came with and without "dope" sprinkles. They actually looked delicious, ringed and iced, purple very-berry, pink candy floss, dark chocolate drizzled with white, and the day's special, rainbow dazzle, in celebration of their LBGTQ+ fundraiser. I hadn't eaten in three hours, and the sweet smell of icing was intoxicating.

"See, not such a bad idea, huh?" Elke nudged me and I grinned back.

"They do look amazing." I selected a sprinkle-free very-berry. Natasha went straight for the sprinkle-free chocolate. We paid separately and waited for Elke.

Elke chose a spiked rainbow-dazzle. "In support of my people, I should really get it for free!" she told the old guy serving her.

The guy grinned. "Rules are rules. All the money from the doughnuts goes to the Gay Straight Alliance, so it really helps us all. Can I see your ID?"

Elke reached into her wallet and pulled out her driver's license. The guy stared at it, looked up at her, then back at her ID.

We noticed the UNDER 21—NO DOPE, NO JOKE sign on the wall.

"Okay, here you go, enjoy!" He handed the license back to Elke, took her cash, and popped the doughnut into a brown paper bag. "Please enjoy responsibly, no driving for three hours."

Elke pointed at Natasha. "No worries. She's the designated driver."

"Don't forget this, one free prerolled joint with every purchase!" He held out a bowl full of them.

Elke grinned like she'd just won the lottery and stuffed one into her pocket.

Outside she burst into laughter. "God, that was fun!"

"You just gave him a fake ID!" Natasha glanced back at the door like the guy might come running after Elke any second.

Elke nodded. "Yep, want me to get you one?"

Natasha tilted her head, considering for a while. "Maybe."

Elke looked at me, as if I was going to ask for one, too. I shook my head. She hadn't changed that much. Being busted for sharing vodka at Yosemite Adventure Camp obviously didn't make her lose her love of risk-taking.

She took one bite of her doughnut and stuffed it back in the bag. "What?" she said, seeing my shocked reaction. "I'm not going to get stoned alone!"

It was so hot and hazy outside, the kind of air that makes your eyes dry and your throat close up. Thank God the Prius had air-conditioning.

"Hey, check this out," Elke pointed at a notice board set between Bud-Bliss and Mike's Diner. It was covered in photos and descriptions of missing people. She pointed to a flyer with a photo of a white teen girl. "She's our age, Harper Swift, missing since July. Can you imagine? There's a ton of them—look: Joshua Jones, missing since January 2022! Still not found. Helen Chen, only fifteen! Missing since June 2019." She wiped some of the dust from the images. "I can't imagine losing someone for that long. And not knowing where they are, what happened to them, if they're still alive."

"Guess it doesn't get changed often," I said. "At least there's some hope all the time you don't know."

"How long can you hold on to that? Like how many years is too many?" asked Elke. "Maybe it's better than knowing for sure you're never going to see them again." Her voice had turned soft.

I had heard something about Elke's dad dying after she left. Some thought it was an excuse for why she'd done what she did. At the time I hadn't cared, but now, the way she was trying to hold it together... I didn't know what to say, so I looked at my feet and waited. "By the way, I'm sorry about your dad," I finally said. "You okay?"

Elke nodded. "I'm fine." She hugged herself and stared at the yellow paint peeling off the diner wall. "It was a long time ago."

"Come on, let's go before we go missing in the Bermuda Triangle of Oregon, and end up on that board!" Natasha was joking, but it was enough to jolt Elke back to her extrovert self.

"Would you rather eat a dope doughnut or smoke a spliff?" she asked as we headed over to the car.

"Dope doughnut. Like, why would you breathe in smoke willingly?"

Elke laughed, "Ah, Lily still so innocent."

With doughnuts consumed and shared, Elke eagerly taking half of Natasha's chocolate one and a large piece of mine, we were ready to set off again. There were still a lot of people in the parking lot, standing in groups around their vehicles, chatting urgently. I noticed cars packed with stuffed trash bags and boxes, and trucks spilling over with suitcases, furniture, and pet carriers. It was like everyone had been evicted at once, and no one had a clue where to move on to.

I watched them as Natasha started the car and began to back out. "Do you think"—I paused as it hit me—"they've been evacuated?"

"Must be from the Wolf Hollow Fire." Elke checked her map app. "It's only five miles away. I guess this is the place to wait it out."

"Most of the time it's a false alarm," said Natasha. She stopped halfway out of the space to let a car go by.

"I can't imagine," Elke said. "But it's those stories where people stay and fight to save their houses that freak me out. I get it, a home you've lived in for years could be gone in seconds, but is it worth your life?" She shook her head. "It's just stuff."

I watched a little girl swinging from her daddy's arms. "Must be hard packing up and getting out with kids."

Natasha backed out again, then glanced over to see where I was looking. There was a slight bump, as if we'd hit a curb.

"Oh, no," said Elke, turning to look out her window. "Did you just hit that red motorcycle?"

Natasha and I looked each other in wide-eyed horror.

Elke opened her door to check. "It's covered in scratches and dents. Maybe the owner won't notice, and even if they do, it's not like it's a bad bump. Anyway, they can't prove it was you."

"But everyone saw!" A couple of people pointed and took out their phones.

"We should leave a note, shouldn't we?" Natasha looked at me, and I nodded.

"We? *You're* the one who backed into it." Elke looked back at the motorcycle, as if it would have somehow gotten out of our way by now.

"What about *my* car?" Natasha asked. "Is it damaged?"

"I didn't notice, but it was only a tap," said Elke. "Just go."

"Yes, go," I said, watching as a young guy with a mop of black hair came out of the diner. He carried a black helmet with a red stripe on it.

Elke saw him, too. "Now, quick now!" She was right. He probably wouldn't even notice unless Natasha panicked.

Natasha put the car back into reverse and jolted it backward. The sound of metal on metal screeched in the air.

The guy ran toward us.

"Go, go, go!" Elke shouted.

Natasha shifted into drive and squealed out of the parking lot. The guy hit the hood with his helmet as she sped past him and yelled something I couldn't make out. By the snarl of his face, it was probably just as well. He raced for his motorcycle.

"Shit, he's coming." Elke knelt in her seat, staring out the rear windshield, "Go! Go! Go! Go! Go!"

"Okay," said Natasha. "How about you calm the hell down?" She sped off, leaving him behind in the parking lot, waiting to merge onto the main road.

Elke and I kept watching behind us. Sure enough the red motorcycle appeared, only moments behind us.

"He's coming, he's coming," I said.

"Speed up," Elke demanded. "Come on. Put your foot down!"

Natasha overtook the truck in front of us, cut into the next lane,

23

and passed the next car on a bend, narrowly missing an oncoming truck in the other lane. Its loud honk vibrated in my spine.

"There, we've lost him now," she said with a hint of excitement in her voice.

But we hadn't. "He's gaining, he's gaining," I said, watching him zoom between lanes as he headed straight for us. "Shit, he's fast!"

"Take a side road," Elke suggested. "This next one before he sees us turn."

"All right, all right!" Natasha swung the car to the left onto a much narrower side road.

"Pull in. Pull in over there!" Elke pointed to a huge red barn. It sat in a field of straw-dry grass, with one long-bearded goat with oversized horns staring mournfully at us through the rickety old fence.

"That's someone's property!" I tried to lock eyes with Natasha in the rearview mirror, but she ignored me and bounced the Prius over the rutted dirt road.

It was a farm—Paradise Farm, according to the bullet-riddled sign. Natasha pulled in behind the barn and turned the engine off. Dust spilled out behind us. There was no way the guy wouldn't figure out where we'd gone. We waited, panting as if we'd been running, not driving. The air was stifling, heat gathering in the car. Sweat trickled down the back of my neck.

"He's not going to bother chasing us if he doesn't know where we've gone. It's not like you really did any damage," said Elke, like she hadn't been at all panicked.

"Shush," said Natasha. "Listen." She cracked her window open, letting in the sounds of birdsong, a tractor somewhere, and a hawk

24

freaking out that we'd come near its nest, but behind that was the faint rumble of a motorcycle. "He's going to find us!" Natasha clutched the steering wheel.

"No, he's not. Even if he drives right past us, he won't see us. Not with that honking big helmet on. It's like horse blinders." Elke grinned in delight.

We listened to the wind and the goat bleating and the soft drone of an airplane overhead.

"See," she said. "We lost him."

Just as Natasha pulled out from the barn, the motorcycle appeared at the top of the road, almost like he'd been waiting for us. She reversed back.

"Do you think he saw us?" She glanced out the window as if she could see him through the barn. "Shit." She bit her lip. "We've trapped ourselves here."

"Wait, stop panicking. I'll go look." Elke got out and walked to the edge of the barn. She peeped out, then shook her head. "He's gone," she yelled. She ran back and yanked the car door open. "I think he's been riding back and forth trying the figure out where we went, but he's not going to waste his time on us. It's not like you crunched it that bad."

"It was pretty bad," I pointed out. "People shoot people for less."

"Maybe in Oakland," said Elke. "Not out here."

I wasn't so sure about that.

"Did you see the signpost?" Natasha started the car back up.

"Yes, but it's not like he's got room to stash a gun on his motorcycle." Elke looked at Natasha, and I swear they were trying not to laugh.

25

Natasha took a slurp of water. "Okay, which way now?"

My heart still raced, but Natasha sounded super calm.

I checked my phone. Jesus, it was five thirty already. "How far to the freeway?" I asked, pulling my hair into a ponytail as if my heart was not racing in my chest.

Elke checked her TRX app. "Keep going over this hill, then take a right and hook up with the main road in a couple of miles. That should easily give us enough distance." She winked at me, and I realized while I had been petrified, Elke had been enjoying the rush.

4

NATASHA TURNED ONTO THE SIDE ROAD AS DIRECTED.
There was no sign of the red motorcycle behind us. That didn't stop
me from staring out the back for a full five minutes before relaxing.
This wasn't so bad. It was better moving than being stuck in traffic
watching red brake lights for miles.

The landscape spun by. The few farmhouses quickly gave way to
farmland, green fields with huge barns, then meadows with woods
behind them. We passed trees with yellow-gold leaves singed with
light brown by the lack of rain and the constant sun, and in a small
clearing, a rainbow of tents with sunburned tops, gathered around a
pond of green algae.

The woods seemed to get closer to the road until there were only
glimpses of pathways between what seemed like rows and rows of
pine trees. The sun hung low in a smoke-tinged sky.

I checked my phone. Finally, a text had come through!

Great. LMK your ETA.

That meant Mom was up and about, but still no results. My arrival time? Sometime after 2:00 a.m. I'd text her when we got back to the freeway. I'd know for sure then. Or would she be worrying waiting for my message, too? I texted back.

ETA 1–2 am don't wait up

There, that would do.

"Is it much farther to the freeway?" I asked. "It doesn't seem like we're on a main road."

"How much farther, Elke?" Natasha tapped her with her elbow, and again I wondered if I was missing something, or if it was just my odd-one-out paranoia.

"Oh sorry, I lost track," said Elke. She checked her phone. "Um, okay, looks like…" She frowned and sucked the air between her teeth. "Mmm, I'm not sure where we are."

A tiny worry line appeared between her eyes. "Do either of you have signal?"

"I have." I pulled my phone back out. "Oh wait, I had it a minute ago." Shit. My text didn't go. "I guess it's gone."

No one had a signal, even though we were on three different data plans.

"You're supposed to keep going until you hit the freeway," Elke explained. "How could we get lost?"

"I thought it was a right turn first, then go until you hit the free-way." I wish I'd paid more attention.

It didn't help that clouds had rolled in, turning the sky a deep

28

purple-gray as dusk fell. Occasionally small side roads came off the one we were on. Roads that led to illegal weed farms, according to Elke, who had an awful lot to say, considering she'd never been there before.

"Like that," she said, pointing to a narrow lane that looked more like a hiking trail than a road. "See the No Trespassing sign with the bullet holes? That's a warning. Sasha's brother, Darius, worked out here. He says never go down those roads alone. Because maybe you're not coming out."

"Oh, please!" I rolled my eyes, but caught a knowing glance go between Natasha and Elke.

"There... Look, gas station to the left. I need to pee. That water went right through me." Elke exaggerated taking the last sip before crushing her can.

The gas station was tiny and hidden, almost like it didn't want to serve anything but locals. Luckily, a lot of people had found it, or we might have driven right by. One pump station served diesel and regular gas. Natasha pulled up parallel to the pump station, missing the line altogether.

A scrawny white teen boy came out from the store to serve us, letting the screen door slam behind him. He came up to Natasha's window. "We're out of regular gas. But I can give you a windshield clean."

"That would be great," said Natasha with a full-on smile. The guy grinned back and went to get the squeegee. So typical that Natasha got service immediately.

"It's so weird, not being allowed to pump your own gas in Oregon," said Natasha, as she looked for coins in the cupholder.

"Oh, you don't tip," said Elke. "Okay, I'm going to the bathroom. Don't drive off and leave me!" She raised her brows at Natasha.

"I'll go inside and ask for directions," I said. Anything to escape whatever weirdness was passing between them.

Twenty people had managed to pack themselves into a shack of a store designed for five. Two women pushed past me with armfuls of chips and water bottles, snapping at their kids that no, they couldn't get a candy bar. An old guy grabbed two cases of beer and almost walked right into me. The constantly ringing doorbell added to the sense of urgency as more people rushed in and out.

I pretended to be looking for a specific candy bar just to be alone for a moment and take a breath. It was so weird being back with Natasha and Elke, trying to read their emotions, the intentions behind their words. It was like they hadn't moved on from middle school and were still in their BFF mode. Whatever, I was well past that.

A couple of young women, barely older than me, huddled together in line while their kids gleefully rearranged the candy bar display.

One of them called over, "Ven, bebe," and the little girl came running back and gave her mom a hug. The other kid carried on playing with the candy.

I listened in on the snippets of conversation in the line.

"This smoke is such a pain. I don't remember it being this bad last year."

"I know. Every year it gets worse."

"Yes, stock up now while you can. Remember last time?"

"Yes, last-minute evacuations. No need to take chances with little ones in tow." Their voices hushed into tense whispers.

A TV above the counter played the local news. *Wolf Hollow Fire has broken across the I-5 freeway. Southbound lanes closed. Detours in place. Expected to reopen in a few hours as fire crews on the scene pushed it back away from the road.*

Good news it wasn't spreading, but still at least a few hours' delay. Shit, I was never getting home.

The gas station clerk leaned over the counter like she was watching a stray cat. "You lost? You don't look like you really want to buy anything." She said it matter-of-factly, more observation than accusation.

"Um, yes, I'll take this." I picked up a stick of jerky from a jar on the counter. "We want to get back to the freeway."

"Then go back the way you came in." Big help. Her face softened. "Follow this road, then turn right onto the freeway. It's not far, six miles." She held out her hand for the money.

I handed her my last dollar bill. "Thanks," I said, stuffing the jerky into my hoodie pocket.

Elke was right outside, reading the notice board. "You okay?"

"I'm fine." Great, I looked as crap as I felt.

"We'll be out of here soon. And that guy is long gone." She tilted her head and smiled. "You always were such a worrier."

Shadows of trees flew by as we got closer and closer to the freeway. I snuggled deeper into my hoodie. Elke tapped her fingers on the dashboard.

Natasha kept glancing at Elke, and when Elke grinned back, it was obvious they were holding a secret between them. I cleared my throat to remind them I was still there.

That day when Elke first appeared as the bright new thing in eighth grade, with her long blond braids, light-brown skin, and big green eyes, wearing a white slip dress with biker boots, she'd looked like she'd come straight off a fashion runway. How could we not fall in love with her?

Natasha had seen Elke and fell instantly into a deep girl crush. She patted the empty chair next to her and smiled her golden Natasha smile, which I have to admit was pretty spectacular.

"Oh, Natasha, that's so kind," said the teacher.

Right. Anyway. That was the past.

Obviously, they were still good friends, but why did I even care? I twirled my ponytail and watched the rows of trees as they got darker and darker, and the world around us seemed to disappear in the twilight haze.

TWILIGHT

5

NATASHA ACCELERATED A LITTLE FASTER. "THERE DOESN'T seem to be so much traffic out here." That was an understatement.

"We were going west, so to get back, we go east. Don't worry, we'll get there," said Elke.

Natasha just laughed. "Not everyone has your 'dropping' skills!"

"Wait, 'dropping'?" I didn't want to ask, but I had to.

Elke turned to me like she was going to whisper a secret. "It's a Dutch thing. When you're about ten, you get dropped at a secret location with a bunch of other kids, with only a flashlight. And you have to find your way home. Oh, and it's dark, like pitch-black, and you're in the middle of a forest. 'Dropping' because you're dropped off and left. It's the most terrifying, most amazing thing I've ever done. Taught me skills for when the signal is out, and you can't use your map apps to find your way home."

"You did that? Your parents abandoned you in a forest and you found your way home? And you thought it was fun?" No wonder she oozed confidence.

"I wasn't abandoned. There were five of us, and if we hadn't got home by morning, our parents would have come to get us. Well, my dad anyway. My mom always thought it was a stupid tradition. But my dad was first-gen Moroccan-Dutch and always wanted me to have the experience he'd missed out on. His dad didn't approve." Elke stopped suddenly as if she'd said too much and sank back into her seat.

My dad was rang in my ear.

"Was he really strict, your grandpa?" I asked.

"Well, I've never really gotten to meet any of that side of my family, except at the funeral." She took a deep breath and looked down at her hands.

Natasha squeezed her arm. Elke flashed her a quick smile, then shook her head, as if shaking out that emotion.

She turned around to me and asked, "Would you rather be a snitch or a thief?"

My breath caught in my throat. Really? She was seriously asking *that*?

"I'll go first. I'd rather be a thief," she added.

"Me too," Natasha agreed.

"How about you, Lily?" Elke turned around to face me. There was no trace of malice in her eyes. But surely, she knew what she'd asked.

"I'd rather do neither," I finally said.

She plowed right on. "Would you rather get lost in a forest or be lost at sea?"

"Forest," said Natasha. "It has to end sometime."

"Same," I added, relieved that the subject had switched so fast. "At least in the forest you don't have to swim all the time."

"Good choice." I felt a strange rush of pride at Elke's approval. "Would you rather—"

36

"Wait," Natasha cut in. "You've got to answer, too."

"Sea," Elke replied. "I'd rather die with the sun on my face than become part of the dank and moldy undergrowth. Picked by off by sharks instead of ants." Nice.

"I hope we get out of here before it gets dark, and the bears and wolves, and whatever else is out there, come to feed on lost travelers." Natasha glanced at the rearview mirror like she was looking for clues.

"They have wolves in Oregon," Elke said. "Wouldn't it be amazing if we heard them howling or actually saw one?" Her eyes sparkled with excitement. I was beginning to realize that adventure was Elke's escape from reality.

I checked my phone. Still no signal. We hadn't even passed a car for miles. "It feels like we're really lost. Perhaps we should go back to that gas station and check directions, buy a map or something." I was practically pleading.

"And risk losing the ten miles we're driven since then?" Elke pouted. "Okay, whatever. Ten more minutes going this way." Elke pressed her nose against the window as if it gave her X-ray vision. "Would you rather be eaten by a wolf or a shark?" she asked.

Seriously? I would rather throw myself out of the car than play this all the way home. I tried not to show my thoughts on my face, but it was getting harder.

"Shark," Natasha answered quickly. "So I don't feel it. Two big bites and I'm gone."

"Wow," said Elke. "I'd rather go down in history as the first Oregon wolf victim. Gore and all."

I shuddered. "I'd rather not be eaten."

"Oh, come on, you can't not play the game. Why do you think we invited you?" Elke caught Natasha's eye. Her mouth twitched as if she was trying not to laugh.

"Okay, then shark." I waited for Elke to demand a reason why, but she didn't. She just nodded.

"Do you realize, Lily, you say yes to things you'd rather say no to?" Elke finally said.

My face burned. I didn't know what to say.

"Just an observation," she said, to make it worse. "No judgment."

"I'm just trying to being nice." I clenched my jaw.

"Yes, leave her alone. We all know what happens when she lets out her inner bitch."

My mouth dropped. I stared at Natasha. Did she really say that? She smiled at me in the mirror. "Joking!"

I stared out the window, trying not to explode. I had to last the whole night with them. And they were still up to their stupid middle-school tricks. Ugh.

Leaves blew across the front windshield as the wind picked up. More clouds gathered, dark as my mood. A yellow barn flashed by. A startled-looking sheep stared at us as we passed. If only we could switch places.

"That's it." Elke stared back at the barn. "Ten minutes is up. You win, Lily. let's go back to the gas station. But first I need to pee. Pull over there." She pointed to a DO NOT TRESPASS sign.

"Wow, demanding much?" Natasha asked, pulling over as requested.

"Again?" I asked.

"Got a problem with that?" Elke asked, all shocked green eyes.

"Nope." I replied.

The Prius bumped along before coming to an abrupt stop at a padlocked gate, with an even narrower lane running behind it. Pine and oak trees lined either side. Their branches hung so low that one scraped the top of the car, like a long fingernail.

Elke unbuckled and swung out the door. "I'm not going alone."

Natasha turned off the engine and asked me, "You coming?"

"I don't need to pee." I crossed my arms.

"Whatever." She turned to Elke. "Why didn't you warn me not to wear this?" Natasha tugged at her black and white daisy-print dress. "If it gets ripped, you owe me a new one."

"Oh my God, you're such a diva." Elke nudged her playfully. "Come on, let's have an adventure." She climbed over the gate, and like a lemming, Natasha followed.

They giggled as they made their way off the road and into the woods. Why go so far to pee? Something felt off. With Natasha's bitchy comments and Elke's would-you-rather crap, it felt safer in the car than out.

I checked my texts. How did anyone live out here with such bad mobile service? I looked around again. That was a long time to spend peeing. I stretched my legs out, then back, then crossed and recrossed them, took out the Oak Canyon College folder, flipped through it and stuffed it back into my bag. I got out of the car in case I could hear them. Maybe they were shouting for help. Maybe they'd been bitten by a rattlesnake. Yeah, not likely.

I called out, "Elke! Natasha!" but only heard the wind whooshing in the leaves.

Then faint at first, then louder, came the rumble of a car engine. As it came closer and closer, the low rumble turned into a rattling roar. It had to be a motorcycle heading right this way. Finally, someone might know where the hell we were.

6

I STOOD BY THE PRIUS READY TO WAVE THE RIDER DOWN.
And there it was, a red motorcycle coming through the haze. A *red*
motorcycle. I ducked, hiding behind the car. Thank God, I hadn't
stood in the road. I took a peek as it got closer. The red stripe on
the black helmet was clear. It was him. The guy we crashed into and
fled from. The guy who chased us. The guy Elke said we'd lost for
sure.

I rushed into the trees, trying not to make too much noise, praying
he wouldn't notice the birds I'd startled. He slowed down. I clambered over the gate and ran. I had to warn Natasha and Elke.

The dirt road on the other side was more like a trail, overgrown
with weeds, leading farther into the forest. Ruts in the hard earth
showed where once upon a time there had been rain. At least one
truck had come through, leaving deep tire marks in the mud. I
blinked, struggling to stop my eyes from stinging in the haze.

A roll of thunder rumbled in the distance. The storm was coming.
The lightning storm we thought we'd miss; we were sure we'd be in
California when it came. I called out to Natasha and Elke, trying to

be loud enough for them to hear, but quiet enough for the sound to not carry back to where the motorcycle rider was. At least I couldn't hear his footsteps following me into the forest.

The thick cloud cover made it seem like twilight already. I guess it nearly was. The sunset was deep orange, the side effect of hazy fire-season skies—beautiful but deadly. The smell of smoke drifted in the air. No wonder my eyes were so dry. I stopped walking. Everything had gone eerily silent.

I took another step. "Hello?" My voice was thin and shaky. I felt like the only living thing in the whole forest.

Leaves rustled like dry bones in the wind; creaking branches murmured. My footsteps crunched on the hard, dry earth. The air was heavy and static. We needed to get the hell out before the dry lightning came and made things worse. In an area this drought- ridden, it would be like throwing a lit match into a puddle of gasoline.

"Elke! Natasha! That guy's here!" I paused to listen. Nothing but my beating heart. "He found the car." He found the car. How did he find us?

The wind picked up, blowing tiny pieces of dust into my eyes. I went flying on a tree root and just about stopped myself from falling to my knees. "Bloody hell!" I sounded like my Scottish gran. I dusted myself off and shouted, "Hey! Natasha, Elke!" My voice got trapped in the thick haze. I shouted again, louder.

They couldn't have gone far. I jogged along the path. They weren't there. I spun around… There wasn't another way to go. Surely, they didn't go this far to pee. They couldn't just disappear. They must have gone farther into the trees.

"Elkeeee????? Natashaaaaaaa!!!" A bird flew out from the tree behind me. There's no way they hadn't heard me calling that loudly. I ran ahead in between the bracken and pine trees, down a fern-lined pathway that turned into something more like a narrowing deer path a few steps in.

"Natasha!" The path dipped ahead. I almost took a step into nothing as the earth suddenly gave way to a crevice in the ground. It was disguised by tangling brambles and ferns. It smelled dank and earthy, like something old and musty lived down there. I trained my phone flashlight on it in case they'd somehow gotten stuck there and were lying unconscious at the bottom. But no. There were just a few bones. Animal bones, I hoped.

Turning off the flashlight made everything seem darker. The trees were more shadow than tree. Any sounds were louder, sharper. The crack of a twig, the scrabble of a small creature. My skin crawled with goose bumps. I was okay, I just needed to find Elke and Natasha.

There was no sun to figure out my direction, and the dying light made it difficult to see where I'd come from. Shit. If I had Elke's dropping skills, I'd be okay. What would she do? She'd look at the stars. But it wasn't quite dark enough and there was nothing but branches overhead. She would know which direction she'd come from and where she was headed. She'd have faith in herself.

I took a deep breath. It was so quiet, hide-and-seek quiet, where you dare not make a sound, or your hiding place will be discovered. "Hello?" I called out. No, they weren't there and wouldn't have heard my faltering voice. Luckily, I didn't need to give them any more reasons than they already had to insist I was the same old worrying Lily.

I shivered. I shouldn't let it get to me, let *them* get to me. I was not that person, hadn't been for a long time.

If they'd cared, they would have come back for me. What if they didn't care? Elke's taunt rang in my ears. *Would you rather be a snitch or a liar?* What if they meant to leave me out here alone? No, nobody would be that cruel.

They left me in the car. They had no idea that guy would turn up. They must have lost their way in the forest, even with Elke's dropping skills.

That's probably how she knew how to start a fire. I shivered. That night, back at Yosemite camp in the pitch-black forest, the whispers, the giggles, footsteps running past my tent, I knew something was happening. Only the popular kids got the invitation from Natasha.

The faint smell of smoke drifted through the air back then, just like now, except then it had been Elke who started the fire, rubbing the sticks together with everyone looking admiringly along. Dancing began to the tinny sound of phone music, and before long someone stepped too close to the fire. And perhaps I did send everyone into a panic when I saw that rogue spark and called out. But it wasn't my fault the rest of Yosemite Adventure Camp was canceled. I didn't start the fire.

I shook the images from my head, no need to go back there. I was a very different person now.

I stepped quietly, stopping every other second to listen.

There it was again, faint giggling. They had come and found me. It was just a joke!

"Hey, guys, over here!" I followed the sound until it became wind flurries in the tree canopies. The ground slanted and I had to run a little, not to slip on the dry leaves. My feet crunched on small stones as it leveled out and widened, and I realized it was not a path, but a dried-up stream.

I shone my phone flashlight to make a path of light to follow. The tree branches drew around me like a tunnel. What if this was it, and I never made my way out, like all those missing people on the flyers? I blinked the tears back from my eyes. I couldn't die here. Mom needed me. I had to get back.

Elke was right. I said yes to things I wanted to say no to. If I hadn't said yes to Dope Donuts, we'd be in California by now. If I hadn't said yes to the ride, I never would have had to face Elke. I'd never have been here at all. But here I was. Lost and alone. *Get a grip.* "You are fine. You are confident. You've got this," I murmured it like a prayer to myself. A prayer that didn't work.

I shivered and looked around. There was no way they'd come this far. They were probably waiting at the car, thinking I'd changed my mind and decided I needed the bathroom after all.

They had to know I was lost by now. They had to be searching. Unless they meant to leave me. My stomach flipped. No, they wouldn't. Would they? Those glances, those taunts, what if my gut was right, and this was all a setup? No, that's impossible. No one would be that mean.

The forest spun around me. Fallen branches tripped me up and ferns reached out to grab my knees. Trees whispered, watching me run and stopping me from breaking free. I shook my head. I was not going to let this freak me out. They would come back for me. They had to.

45

I plummeted through the undergrowth, into brambles. The farther I got, the more I thought I'd heard their voices, or something like footsteps. There was a gunshot. I fled in the other direction. If there were hunters out there, they could mistake me for an animal.

I yelled out. "Over here! I'm over here!" like a warning. Another roll of thunder rumbled.

I thrashed on, with no idea where I was going. Elke and Natasha had to be back at the car. There was no way the motorcycle guy would have waited around this long.

It felt like the path was going downhill, which hopefully meant it led to the road. There was a clearing ahead, a little circle surrounded by trees. A couple of large logs were positioned like benches around a firepit. A couple of crumpled Draper IPA cans glinted in the dirt. I had to be closer to the road if this was a drinking spot. It didn't matter if it was the right road, as long as there was a way out.

And finally, there was a gate, just like the gate we'd climbed over when we made our way in. Only this gate had a sign across it saying WARNING. FIRE ROAD. DO NOT BLOCK. I must have come out the other side.

I checked my phone. Six thirty. I'd only been lost thirty minutes; it had felt like hours. But that was still a long time to lose a friend in the woods. They must be freaking out. I followed the dirt road out from the woods, and finally there was a real road, cracked and potholed but an actual paved road. I almost cried with relief but shook it off and ran along it until I saw the outline of the Prius. I'd never been so pleased to see that crappy old car in my entire life.

As I got closer, I saw a flash of red next to it. The motorcycle was still there. I froze. In the dim smoky light, leaning against the car, the guy was chatting with Elke and Natasha. *Chatting.* WTF?

I stepped back behind the trees, took a deep breath, then peeked around again. Elke touched the guy's arm while she leaned in to say something.

He said something back that made Natasha throw her head back with laughter and squeal, "OMG, Darius!" Darius. He was *Darius,* the one they'd been texting.

It was all so intimate, so comfortable. Like watching old friends. Old friends, playing a cruel prank on a common enemy.

7

THIS WAS IT. WHILE I'D GOTTEN LOST TRYING TO FIND AND warn them about the "motorcycle guy" being back, they were hanging out with him. He was their friend! They weren't bothered about me at all. Or maybe they were, and they hoped I'd get lost— for real. I guess I should count myself lucky they were still there. Maybe it would have been better if they'd left. Hitchhiking home with a stranger had to be safer than riding with them.

I'd been gone over half an hour, and they were stood around like they'd bumped into an old friend at the supermarket. Screw this. How long had they been planning it? Was everything part of the plot—the crash, the doughnuts, the ride offer? How did he know where to find them?

Stars flickered in the corner of my vision. I bent over to breathe, deep breaths in and out.

When Elke peeked around the barn, was she actually waving to him, showing him where we were? Those texts to Darius... They had to be part of the setup, but what had I done to deserve this?

My head was on fire. It was so reckless and immature. They

obviously hadn't moved on from middle school at all. I couldn't face them this angry. My fists were so tight I might never be able to unclench them. I couldn't speak.

No way was I going back in that car. I'd rather walk home. They wanted me gone, I'd be gone. I'd hide and watch, and listen, and see how they liked it when their careful plans spun out of control.

Another roll of thunder echoed across the sky. One Mississippi, two Mississippi, three Mississippi, still no flash of lightning, so it was still miles away. Plenty of time to mess with their heads.

They were so engrossed with each other, it was easy to get closer without them noticing.

"Oh my God and that U-turn... I was sure she was going to figure out by then that we were just randomly driving around pretending to be lost when we were just waiting for the right time." I could hear the grin in Natasha's voice. Yes, it was all so very funny.

"I almost lost you. I was like wait, wasn't that the gas station? And then you were still parked there so I had to zoom by and hope she didn't notice." Darius's voice was so warm and friendly, nothing like the persona he'd played as the angry guy we crashed into earlier. But there he was laughing at me with the rest of them.

"She was in the store, asking for directions!" Elke cracked up laughing.

Bitches. What the hell was wrong with them?

Darius coughed and kicked the ground with his boot. Elke hummed to herself. No more laughter now. Perhaps it was finally sinking in. I wasn't coming back. I wondered if that had happened to any other lost girls. Had they been deliberately lost, or had they lost themselves? A forest full of lost souls. My skin crawled with goose bumps.

"I wonder if Lily's really lost," Natasha said a little more quietly.

"Isn't that the point?" Darius asked. "To scare her a little?" He cleared his throat. "How long are you planning to stick around and wait for her?"

"As long as it takes," Natasha replied. "Unless she's out on the main road hitching a ride."

"The storm's coming in, supposed to be a big one. I'm not staying out here all night. I've played my part." There was a clicking sound like Darius was playing with his helmet strap. Getting impatient.

"Maybe you played it too well. What if she totally freaked out, charged into the woods, and hurt herself?" Elke asked. "It's been a while now."

What if indeed? I could be dead by now, like a real life would-you-rather game. Would you rather Lily fell down a ravine, or was eaten by wolves? I wriggled a little to stop my feet from falling asleep and cracked a branch. I froze, but Darius carried on clicking his helmet, while Elke paced in front of the car.

Natasha huffed. "It's almost night. She's not going to stay out here in the dark. She's got to have realized we ditched her by now. I bet she's already gone back to the gas station and gotten a ride home. You know how she overreacts."

I overreact? How the hell would she know? We hadn't said more than hi in years. And how was I supposed to react to being ditched in a forest, in the dark, in a storm? Roll over and laugh?

Elke opened the car door and rummaged around in the back.

Probably raiding my bag, because why not? "Pranking Lily is one thing. Deserting her is another altogether. I'm not doing that." So, Elke did draw the line somewhere. Not that it meant anything. They were all up to their necks in the let's-freak-Lily-out prank.

"Of course, I intend to take her home. I'm not a monster!" Natasha backtracked.

"That's debatable." Darius said it under his breath but if I could hear it, Natasha could, too.

"Look, she left her bag. She wouldn't do that if she was hitching a ride." Too late to feel sorry for me now, Elke.

A growl of thunder rattled too close. I almost stood up right then, but what would I say? "I've been watching you and I hate you?" Making us all another half hour late wasn't exactly payback for pranking me. No, I needed something more.

"Guys, come on. We have to go in after her. She's been in there way too long." Elke almost sounded like she was pleading, and I always thought Natasha did everything Elke asked her to. "I know you hate her, but that is heartless." Wow, hate me for what?

"You go after her. With your skills, I'm sure you'll find her in seconds." Natasha got back into the car. "Come on, you know she's not still in there."

"Elke's right," said Darius.

"Oh, that's okay then," Natasha snapped back. What was going on between them?

Sheet lightning flashed above us. My heart stopped. For a second, I thought they'd seen me.

"That's come early." Darius paused like he was watching the sky.

"Why don't you take the car back to the main road in case she somehow came out up there, and is trying to hitch a ride, like you're so sure she is. I'll ride around all the side roads. Hell, I'll even go back to the gas station and see if anyone's seen her. And Elke, you go into the woods and call for her."

"Who made you the boss? And thanks for giving me the easy part," Elke said sarcastically. "What if I get lost?"

"I thought that was your thing, Dutch orientation skills or something. It's just a little forest. You won't get lost," said Darius.

"Thanks for mansplaining that," said Elke.

"He has got a point though. This was fun, but it's getting booooring." It was unlike Natasha to turn on Elke that fast. Or maybe it wasn't. Maybe she'd changed, too.

A clap of thunder knocked against the mountains.

"Wow, that's close. Let's do this if we're doing it," said Elke.

Shit, my cue to exit. I slipped between the trees—just far enough to be out of sight, but within hearing range, so I could watch Elke walk back into the woods.

I waited for the roar of the motorcycle and the almost silent whoosh of the Prius before leaving my hiding place completely. I even stood on the side of the road watching, making sure they'd both disappeared and didn't change their minds. Then I walked carefully, following Elke's stomping bootsteps ahead. The smoky haze gave the dusk a sepia tinge. Elke coughed and made me immediately want to do the same. I held it tight in my throat until my eyes watered. It came out as a yelp.

"Hello?" she called, "Lily, are you there?"

I whimpered like a wounded animal. She spun around and ran back toward the road. I waited until I was behind her.

"Help, help! Elke! Natasha! Help!" I called it very faintly, as if I was faraway and barely alive. Which I could have been!

She ran right past me, farther into the woods. I sat and waited. It's not like she would get lost, because as she couldn't stop telling everyone, she had skills and knew exactly how to find her way around. It wouldn't take Elke long to find her way back. I needed to get her lost.

8

"LILY?" ELKE SOUNDED LIKE SHE'D GONE IN REALLY FAR.
"Lily?"

I ran toward her, crashing around tree trunks and undergrowth, slipping on dry leaves. Prickly ferns scraped against my jeans. I stopped to catch my breath. Running was way harder in the hazy air. A clap of thunder pounded right above me. I waited to feel the rain, but there was none. Of course, there would be none. It was a dry storm, just a gush of wind and a rattle of leaves.

Perhaps I'd sounded like whatever was thrashing around when I was lost in there before. Elke might even feel like she was being watched. Maybe she was even scared. I hoped so.

"Lily, is that you?"

Hah, she was scared. I crept a little bit farther away and called out, "Elke, help me!" Letting my voice trail off dramatically at the end. Then moved farther away before calling again, "Elke, help!"

"I'm coming!" She sounded frantic. My plan was working.

She rushed toward where I had been. "Lily, Lily?"

Every time I ran away a little, staying low behind ferns, darting behind tree trunks, luring her deeper into the woods and farther away from the car. Calling her name anytime she seemed hesitant to follow. At one point she rushed so close to me, I slipped on the dry ground and, in my haste to get out of her sight, grabbed hold of a tree trunk and grazed my hand.

"Shit." I shook the pain out.

"Lily? Where the fuck are you?" Nice and to the point.

"Elke!" I yelled it through cupped hands this time, diffusing the sound and sending my voice everywhere at once. A flash of sheet lightning spilled across the sky.

"Lily!" She crashed away from me.

It was getting hard to follow her. The last thing I needed was to lose her. And that lightning wouldn't stay in the clouds for long.

"Elke, Elke over here!" I forgot to sound fragile and afraid. "Help!" I added half-heartedly.

She turned and came running back toward me. There was a thump. Then silence. Crap, oh crap, don't be hurt. There was payback and there was vengeance. I wanted this to hurt, without actually hurting her. I backtracked to where I last heard her. Running in the dying light through a forest is not smart. I went flying over a bump and landed in a thorn bush that stabbed like needles into my knees.

"Shit!" Oops, I clasped my mouth shut.

"Lily? Lily? Is that you?" Elke was so close.

"Yes, here!" I shouted while I inspected my knee, pulling out thorns by flashlight.

"Wow, you look like a ghost," Elke said, creeping up beside me. "Are you okay?"

I scowled at her. "What do you think?" I picked out the last thorn. "How should someone lost in the woods look?"

We stood staring at each other, unsure what to say. Did she even realize I wasn't lost and had lured her in? Her knees were muddied and her cheek had a trickle of blood where she'd scratched it on something.

A line appeared between her eyes while she figured out what was going on. "Were you even lost?" she finally asked.

"Were you even worried?" I shot back.

"What do you mean? Of course, I was, or I wouldn't have come after you."

"Oh really, so you did go for a pee, again?" I cocked my head in fake concern.

"Ahh," she nodded. "So, you figured it out?" She didn't even sound annoyed. "How did you get so lost in here?"

"I wasn't lost." I couldn't stand her thinking I'd been lost all that time and she'd found me. "I ran in after you to tell you the motorcycle guy had shown up, though apparently he isn't even that big a threat." My words came out like sparks. "I was worried you'd got hurt, or something, and then I noticed how quiet it was, because you weren't there at all. So, I got lost, for a little while. Then I found my way out. Because maybe I'm not quite as pathetic as you both seem to think I am."

"I know you're not pathetic. You got me expelled. That takes balls." Elke crossed her arms.

"Wait, what? All this was for that?" I glared at her.

She shrugged.

"I don't care what you think of me. I'm not trying to impress you."

"Oh, come on, Lily. You were always trying to impress me." She narrowed her eyes.

My face flushed. "I don't care about you, Elke. I never have, and I never will."

She rolled her eyes. "Jesus, you are so dramatic."

"I'm dramatic? You are awful. The crash, the U-turn, the dough-nuts, all for this? I hope it was worth it! I'm glad you got expelled." I took a deep breath. "So, for some stupid thing that happened way back in middle school, you abandoned me in the forest." I shook my head. I still couldn't believe it.

"It's okay. It never would have gotten to that," said Elke.

"It wouldn't have got to *that*?" I spoke with absolute precision. "So, you wouldn't have abandoned me. You were just going to wait for me to find my way out, giving me the scare of my life, for something that happened when we were twelve?" I glared at her. If looks could kill, I'd shot her down.

"Did you never think about what you'd done?" Elke asked.

"I didn't host a secret party. I didn't start the fire." I couldn't believe she was blaming me for something that was her fault.

Another sheet of lightning flashed across the sky.

"I'm sorry." Not sorry. "There, is that what you wanted?" I was sorry at the time. It was awful. I had no idea things would spin out of control so fast. It's not like I wanted Elke to get expelled. But if Natasha still blamed me, she needed to get a life. I was done with being sorry now.

"I was twelve. It was an overreaction. I thought I was doing the right thing. It wasn't like you were totally innocent." Or innocent at all. "We could have just talked about it, you know, like grown-ups!"

"It wasn't really planned," Elke said. "It just fell into place. It's your mom's fault really."

"Oh, don't you dare!" I took a step toward her.

"Okay, okay," she held her palms up. "It was Natasha. It came to her when your mom called hers and asked for the favor. I mean, no apology for four years, then a favor, really? When else were we ever going to get you back?"

"Get me back? I'm not even the same person." I brushed away tears of frustration.

"Red streaks and makeup don't make you a different person. You're still acting like it was nothing to do with you. You can't just bury the past."

Why not? It had worked perfectly well so far. "Whatever." This payback was not going according to plan. "This was a really stupid idea."

"Come on, you seriously can't be that surprised... Natasha wanting to give you a ride? Being nice to you?"

"I thought you might have forgotten, or at least forgiven." I don't know what I thought. It was more of a hope that it was all over finally. "I was grateful. How lame is that?" Really lame. Great, now I felt like I was in middle school again. Back there in the loser section. Only I wasn't. I shook my head. "Anyway, it's over. I hate you. You hate me. Even." I didn't hate her. Not really. I just wanted out of there.

Then it hit me. "You know what, Natasha and Darius haven't even come looking for you. You've been gone what, half an hour? Looks like they've abandoned you, too."

Elke looked horrified, genuinely scared.

"This was ridiculous. I'm sorry. I'm sure I'm wrong." I scratched my head. "This whole ride, seeing you again, and everything else."

"It's a lot." Elke tilted her head as if she wasn't sure if it was a statement or a question.

"Yep." I let out a huge sigh.

"Truce?" Elke held out her hand. I wanted to say no, but I nodded and shook it. "So, do you know the way out of here?" Elke asked.

"Umm, I think I've gone a bit offtrack, but you can get us out, right?"

"Yeah, right." She stared into the dark ahead of us.

EVENING

9

"DO YOU RECOGNIZE ANY LANDMARKS?" ELKE RAISED
her brows.

Her violet hair glowed in the dimness, making it easier to see her.
My companion in night hiking. It was less scary to be lost with someone than to be alone. Even if that was not someone I wanted to be
with.

My feet crunched on the dry bracken as I went. I was trying to be
careful, but it was almost impossible to see where my feet were going.
The ground was covered in dry stuff, roots, rocks, earth, leaves. In
the haze and dark, it all looked the same. "When I was here before, I
found a campsite in a dell."

"A dell?"

"Like an open space that dips a little in the ground, like a hollow
or a tunnel—a fancy Scottish term." I stopped to take an extra breath.
"Or British, whatever. I always assumed fairies lived there from the
folktales my gran used to read me."

"Ah, nice. I doubt there are any here." She stopped to look at the
sky again. It flashed with sheet lightning on command. "Shit, let's

speed it up in here. Forests are not a good place to be in a storm." She ran a little. "Come on, keep up."

"'Coming!" I hurried after her.

Thunder rolled around above us. We ran on another few minutes without talking. Until finally out of breath, I had to stop.

"Wait up," I called out feebly. "Elke!"

"Don't panic, I'm right here." She bent over, huffing beside me.

"Can you imagine if you'd left me and I didn't find my way out?"

"I told you already, it was never going to come to that. Just let it go, or I will leave you here!" She grinned to let me know she didn't mean it, but her eyes were looking behind me for someone else, or at something else.

"What?" I turned quickly. There was nothing there.

"I don't know. I just got that feeling. At first, I thought maybe Darius and Natasha were playing a double trick because you never know."

"Yes, you never know with Natasha."

Elke shook her head. "She's not mean. She just gets carried away sometimes, excited. She's harmless though."

I rolled my eyes. Here we go again, defending Natasha like she was the only one with feelings. Yep. "Maybe to you."

"You said truce," Elke warned. She stopped for a second and glanced around. "It still feels like we're being watched. Let's keep moving. I'm surprised they haven't come to find us."

"'She just gets carried away.'" I paused to let her hear how lame her own words sounded. "I expect she hasn't noticed you're even missing. She's too busy flirting with Darius." Yes, I wanted it to hurt. Just like she hurt me.

"She is not." Elke flicked her hair. "Natasha will have noticed and be worried and be looking for me."

"Right, so where is she? Oh, maybe she's calling for you, and we can't hear her because you're too busy defending her!"

I felt Elke's scowl even though I could hardly see her face in the dim light.

"This whole prank doesn't feel like a harmless joke. Getting lost is not harmless; it's reckless." I tried to keep my voice calm. "Especially when there's high fire danger and a thunderstorm."

She didn't even try. "Then why did you lure me back in!" The truce was officially over.

The first streak of lightning struck the ground. The stench of scorched wood filled the air.

"Run, run, run!" I yelled.

A small rodent scurried by my feet as I ran. I shuddered and raced on. I didn't even care if Elke was following. There was the campsite. No, it was just another empty patch. Shit. I stopped still and Elke ran right into me.

She jerked away and stepped into a thorn bush. "Crap. That better not be poison ivy." She screwed her nose up. "This is a shit road trip." Her T-shirt clung to her. She was as sweaty as me.

"I'm aware. Maybe we should listen for them."

"Or shout. Natasha! Darius!" Elke stumbled on ahead.

"Natasha, Darius!" I joined in, not that I wanted to see them; I just wanted to get the hell out of there. I don't know why I didn't make my own way back. Oh yeah, I do. Elke was supposed to be an expert.

When I reached Elke, she was twirling around, trying to figure which way to go. She wiped her eyes with both palms. "It's so dark. It all looks the same."

There was a crash ahead. We stood there, frozen, waiting for whatever it to emerge from the trees. Running was pointless. I held a rock in my right hand ready to brain a bear, or at least throw the rock at it. I swallowed. My throat stuck to itself. I could see silver specks before my eyes, like before you faint. Elke grimaced, grabbed a stick, and we were ready—terrified but ready. So not ready.

"Hey, they're here!" Darius emerged, grinning like a Cheshire cat. "I found them! They're alive!"

He said it like a joke, and I didn't care. I was so relieved to be found.

"Oh my God. You found us! We were so lost!" Elke hugged him.

"I knew we'd find you," he said, all smiles and big brown eyes.

"Yes, thanks so much!" I said. Finally, let's go already.

He held my arm. "Are you okay? I never meant for you to be lost for so long. I mean, it wasn't my idea, but if I'd known all this would take so long, and in a storm..." He gestured with his hands. "It's a terrible idea!"

"Yeah, yeah," said Natasha coming up behind him, sweeping her hair off her face. "No one meant for you to be lost this long. I mean, wow, of all the days to take a ride through Oregon, right?"

I stood there with my mouth open. This was her fault! "This didn't just *happen*." I scowled at her. "I only got lost because of your stupid prank."

"And I only got lost because *she* tricked me back." Of course, Elke wouldn't admit to getting lost, too.

I shut my mouth and glared at Natasha. "So, can we go now?"

"Of course," Darius replied and twirled the car keys in his hand. He grinned at Natasha as he made them spin faster.

"Darius, stop it!" Natasha made a snatch for them. "The last thing we need is you dropping them!" She gripped them tightly in her fist and pushed past him.

Elke made a face at Darius. He shrugged.

"Hopefully you know the way out," Elke said doubtfully.

"More than you do even with your 'special skill set.'" Natasha walked a few steps, then stopped. "See! You were right by the road and didn't even know it!" And she laughed.

I glanced at Elke. Her jaw was clenched, like she was holding everything in as she followed Natasha to the car. And then she couldn't. "How long was I gone before you noticed I might be lost, too?"

Natasha shrugged. "I don't know. A bit. Honestly, Elke, I thought you could look after yourself. I'd have died if anything really happened to you. And look here you are, fine."

"*Fine?*" said Elke.

That *fine* hit like a slap. I got into the car fast, before things fell apart again.

"Hey," Darius called over. "We're all tense. Am I right?" He stared at Natasha, who clamped her mouth tight.

"Right," said Elke. She opened the front passenger door. "Are you okay in the back?" As if she actually gave a shit.

I shrugged. "I'm good." It was better to be alone for a while—a long while, assuming we made it to the freeway. God, that stupid prank had wasted almost two hours. Eight hours home. Home to Mom's test results. Hopefully she'd be asleep by the time I got back. One silver lining to arriving home at dawn instead of in the wee early hours, as my gran called them.

I didn't want to be there. I wasn't wanted there. I might as well have disappeared into the forest. No, Elke did come in after me. I caught her eye in the side-view mirror. She gave a small nod. I nodded back. Okay. We were almost at truce again. Luckily, I wouldn't have to deal with either of them anymore. I could just go to sleep, or at least pretend, slumped in the back seat. I crossed my legs, took a sip of flat cherry water, and clicked my seat belt in.

Darius started up his motorcycle and lined up behind us. He shouted something.

"What?" Natasha yelled out the window at him.

He pointed to the road ahead. She nodded and we set off, closely following Darius on his motorcycle, along a windy, unpaved road that seemed to be leading us straight toward an amber glow.

10

"IS THAT FROM THE WOLF HOLLOW FIRE?" I ASKED, POINTing at the glowing sky. "Shouldn't it be out by now?"

"It always looks worse at night," said Natasha. "It looks brighter in the dark."

"Right, but that smoke plume looks bigger than before." I knew what distant fires looked like. And the glow didn't get bigger unless the fire did.

"Yes, because we're heading toward it," said Natasha, as if I had no clue how perspective worked.

"It's miles away. It's not like we're in danger. No need to panic," Elke added.

"I'm just thinking of the freeway on the ride home, if the detour's still there, or whatever." Jesus, why was I justifying myself?

"Darius knows where he's going," said Elke. "Stick of gum?" And she handed me a stick of Juicy Fruit.

I rolled my eyes but took it, rolled it up, and popped it in my mouth. That flavor took me right back to middle school.

Her eyes locked with mine. "People say stupid things when they're scared."

"What like, truce?" I asked.

She frowned. "No, like just things." She broke off as Natasha leaned in to listen.

"What, so you're besties now?" Natasha asked sarcastically.

"No, no we're—" I started.

"Not," Elke finished.

I folded in to myself, arms and legs crossed, face against the window. Hunched against the world.

"What happened back there?" Natasha whispered to Elke, like I wouldn't hear.

"Yes, what happened? Where were *you*?" Elke shot back.

"I seriously thought you'd be okay. Come on, when have I ever let you down?" Natasha squeezed Elke's arm. "You know I'm always here for you."

Elke pulled her arm away. "That's exactly my point. You weren't, and then you laughed." Wow, Elke was so pissed at Natasha that she wasn't even going to remind her that it was my fault she got lost in the woods.

"I was just relieved, and it came out badly." Natasha bit her lip. "I'm sorry I didn't notice how long you'd been gone in the woods. I really am."

We drove in silence. Perfect. Like strangers trapped in a car together. Not that it mattered.

Thunder grumbled over the mountains and a crack of lightning split the sky, followed closely by another.

"I thought we'd be out of here by now." Natasha's knuckles whitened as she gripped the steering wheel tighter.

"We'll be out of here soon, as long as we don't get lost again," Elke said. "Accidentally or deliberately."

"If Lily hadn't tricked you back into the woods, none of us would still be here anyway," Natasha said with a flourish of a hair flick.

"If you hadn't done the stupid prank in the first place, we'd almost be home by now!" Okay, halfway home, but still.

"If you hadn't pretended Elke getting expelled was nothing to do with you, we wouldn't have wanted to get you back," Natasha said, like it was a perfectly reasonable thing to do. It was becoming increasingly obvious that she was the one with the bigger grudge.

"Seriously, you needed to pay me back for something that happened four years ago by trying to scare me in the woods." I frowned. "You couldn't have talked to me anytime afterward instead?"

"You ran every time I came near you." Natasha swerved the car a little too close to the edge as she hit the next corner.

Knots wriggled in my stomach. "I knew you hated me, so what was the point? Anyway, we were twelve!" Being trapped there with them was like being dragged back to eighth grade—the stupid Yosemite Adventure Camp, that secret party, the charged excitement, the terrible end. I pushed it all down and clenched my jaw.

"Yes, I've been waiting four years for you to show in some tiny way that you're sorry for screwing up Elke's life."

"Okay, let's just admit it all got a little out of control," said Elke. "And recognize we were all responsible. Natasha, you don't need to fight my battles anymore" Elke turned the music up, drowning out any answer Natasha might give. Fine. I'd rather not talk anyway.

A faint house light and a faint car beam came into view from the

71

valley below as we turned another corner. Not totally alone then. Another clap of thunder boomed through the mountains, swiftly followed by a shatter of lighting that spread like a network of veins across the sky.

"I'm glad we're not in the woods now." Elke stared at the storm.

"We get them almost every year like this. Still can't get used to them," Natasha admitted as another bolt of lightning cracked the sky in two.

It was intense, but I couldn't take my eyes off the orange glow to the right of us. I had a sinking feeling we were headed the wrong way. Surely, we should be entering the freeway south of the fire to bypass any detours.

"Hey," Natasha snapped. "Elke, turn that down. I want to hear my app when we get into range." Perhaps Natasha had the same worry as me. She took another sharp turn, following the red lights of Darius's motorcycle.

Elke turned it down and checked her phone. "You don't need your app. You're following Darius. Don't you trust him?"

"It doesn't feel right to me either," I admitted.

"I just don't like relying on anyone, that's all." Natasha gripped the steering wheel harder as the wind buffeted the car from side to side. "Except you," she added. "I know I can rely on you." She glanced hopefully at Elke.

Elke tapped the dashboard. "Eyes on the road." And pointed at the curve ahead.

Natasha sped into it, skidding as she took the sharp corner. At this rate, we were going to plunge over the mountain edge.

I gripped the seat. *Sorry, Mom.* What if the worst news happened, and I wasn't there to help Mom take it? I closed my eyes and took a deep breath. There was nothing else I could do.

For the next few miles, the road was narrow and covered in gravel, so the wheels kept slipping and spinning as we got higher and higher. At one point the car slid backward. We leaned forward, as if that would make a difference, but the car got the hint and kept on moving in the right direction.

Elke bounced her seat into my knees. The sky glowed with lightning as it splintered relentlessly around us.

I leaned forward. "Do you think Darius really knows where he's going?" I asked.

"Better than you do," Natasha shot back.

"Just because he's your 'special friend' doesn't mean he's invincible," said Elke.

"I know that, but I trust him." That was Natasha, loyal to the end, until she found someone better.

The Wolf Hollow smoke plume was spreading. No matter how far we drove, it seemed to be reaching out to us. We couldn't be that far from the freeway, but the road seemed to be twisting upward, and I doubted it was going to connect with the I-5 up there. I swallowed. Great time to get carsick. I would not be sick. *I would not be sick.* "Can we pull over a sec?"

Natasha sighed. "Just hold it down until the next curve so I don't lose sight of Darius."

I nodded, scared to open my mouth in case it flew out.

"Are you really going to puke? I thought it was a joke." Elke turned around to me. I was tempted to hurl all over her. "Oh my God, you're going green! I thought that was just a saying, and here you are proving it!"

I gave her a sarcastic smile and she quickly turned back around.

I don't know why I was so riled by her. For a moment back there when we were both lost, it felt like there was something, a spark between us, friendship, trust. Now it was like it never happened. She was back to her deflecting self, where everything was such a laugh, and she was so much wittier and more adventurous than anyone else, or maybe just so much *more*.

I coughed. It was the haze that made my eyes tear up.

"You okay back there?" Natasha asked. "Not dying or anything?"

I nodded, keeping the cough tight in my throat.

Natasha drove steadily on, face pushed closer to the windshield, like that would help her see around corners. A twig shot out and hit one of the windows. I shrieked as Natasha swerved and sped straight toward the mountainside before braking into a screaming halt.

"Oh my God!" said Elke. "That was close!"

I nodded in agreement, too shook up to speak.

11

"SHIT! ARE WE STUCK?" ASKED ELKE.

Natasha tried to reverse. The wheels spun, but the car wasn't moving.

"What the hell?" Elke jumped out, phone flashlight in hand.

Natasha called after her, "Can you see anything?"

Elke shrugged. "It's not like I'm a car mechanic or anything. Guess we'll have to push."

As we all got out of the car, Darius came roaring back on his bike. He must have been keeping a closer eye on us than Elke gave him credit for.

The front right tire was stuck in a crack in the side of the road where Natasha had swerved.

"Oh, nasty," said Darius when he saw it. "Okay, don't worry, we'll get out of here." He took off his helmet and shook out his hair.

"Don't worry? Do I look worried?" Natasha tutted, then checked the damage with the rest of us.

"Ahh, easy fix." Elke leaned against the car.

I joined her, hands on the trunk, ready to push. Natasha got back into the car to steer.

"Hey," I called to Darius, who was busy staring at Natasha. "You helping, or what?"

He hurried to help. We pushed, and then turned around and shoved with our backs, heels digging into the dirt, our legs getting hit with sharp little stones as the wheels spun. The front tire kept almost rolling out, then falling back in.

"I know, I know!" Elke practically jumped up and down. "Hold up, Natasha!" She dove into the back of the car and came out with a floor mat. "Put this as close to the front wheel as possible, to help it gain traction and get over that hole."

I rushed to help her get it in place, then back to the Prius to push.

"Ready here," Darius yelled.

Natasha pressed down on the accelerator, the car jolted forward, rocked back, then rolled a tiny way forward and broke free.

"Yay!" I forgot myself and grinned at Elke.

She grinned back. "Let's go then!"

But we needed to hurry. Thunder rolled all around us. From where we were on the mountain, we could see lightning striking every few seconds. And far off, but so bright, the golden glow of the Wolf Hollow fire.

A flash of lightning helped us hurry back into the car.

"How much farther? I thought you said it was close." I called to Darius through my opened window. "Do you even know where we're going?"

"Relax, we're going south to connect with the freeway below the holdup." He pulled his motorcycle up from the dirt. "It's still the quickest way."

"You sure about that?" Natasha asked. She held up her phone. "As soon as I get a signal, I'm following my app."

Darius rolled his eyes and muttered something under his breath.

"What was that?" Natasha snapped.

"I said, 'Then you're a fool.'"

"Do not *evv-ver* call me a fool." Natasha shot him a dagger side-eye.

Darius didn't even flinch. "Don't be one then."

Elke and I shared a WTF glance. It was a Natasha-Darius standoff.

"Shall we get going?" Elke suggested hesitantly.

Natasha nodded her head. "Yes, let's. Sorry, Elke. It's not you. It's this situation getting to me." She stared at Darius.

"It's fine," said Elke in a way that suggested it wasn't going to be fine at all.

We drove on, following Darius, for what seemed like ten miles but was probably two.

Headlights came up behind us. Natasha slowed way down and moved as far over as she could. A white four-by-four squeezed past carrying what looked like huge containers of water.

Elke scrunched her nose. "This haze is getting worse. I can't wait to be out of it."

"I'm trying the best I can," Natasha snapped. Then she sighed. "I'm sorry it's just…a lot."

Elke nodded and I stared out the window. Natasha had never been great in stressful situations. Awesome at creating them, terrible dealing with the fallout. I guess I wasn't much better.

"So, how come Darius knows his way around here, anyway?" I asked.

"He interned at a winery in Newberg, Oregon, wine country," Natasha replied.

"He makes wine?" I don't know why it was so shocking.

"You expected weed, right?" Elke's eyes wrinkled at the corners.

I smiled back. Wait, what was I doing? She wasn't my friend. She'd proved that enough times already.

"You probably knew him in middle school," said Natasha. "He was in eighth grade when we were in sixth."

Back when we used to be friends, or maybe it was just me that remembered that.

"Nope." I shrugged. "I don't remember him." I'd only been focused on my friendship with her. "I don't look back at middle school much." Or ever.

"Not even at the big things that happened, like the fire at adventure camp?" Elke turned to face me.

"I prefer to leave the past in the past," I said. Unlike some.

"You never look back and acknowledge your mistakes?" Elke narrowed her eyes at me.

"Why should I? I'm not that same person now." I flicked a stray hair off my face.

"You sure about that?" I could feel Elke's gaze burning my cheeks as she waited for my answer, but I stared down at my hands in silence.

"In high school you can go from being nobody to 'most likely to be famous' in less than a year. But others cling to their sad-sack old selves and never evolve into anything. Never grow from their mistakes," Natasha observed.

Elke joined in. "People reinvent themselves from one school to the next, nothing wrong with that, especially if you were ashamed of the person you used to be. Right, Lily?"

I think she meant this as an olive branch, but it felt awfully like a dig, so I just gave a curt nod. All the feelings of eighth grade came rushing back. The loneliness. The anger. The revenge. It was a nightmare I didn't want to revisit. My insides felt tangled up like I'd swallowed a vine and it was tightening around all my organs at once. I needed to get out of there, out of that car.

"Can you pull over? Pull over, please?" I asked.

Natasha frowned but slowed down. I yanked open the door before she even fully stopped and leaned out the door, head bowed ready. I swallowed down the bile. It came right back up. It was no good. I lurched from the car to puke on the gravel, my silhouette highlighted by the car beams. *Great, very attractive.* Another bout came up again. *Shit.* I wiped my face on my sleeve, shivered, and got back in the car. I looked at them all staring at me.

Great. My throat felt like I'd swallowed sawdust. I drank the last drop of flat water and scrunched up the can.

Darius circled his motorcycle around, seeing us stop. "You okay?" he asked.

Elke tried not to smile, because me puking was so funny. Natasha just sighed. She'd seen this before, after Mom was first diagnosed. I'd held everything in, and this was my body's way of letting it all out. Gross, but true.

Darius removed his helmet and wiped the sweat from his forehead. "I should drive behind you since you keep stopping all the time. Unless you were deliberately trying to lose me." He cocked his head at Natasha.

"You'd know it if it was deliberate." She turned to me. "You sure you're okay?"

I nodded. I didn't want to talk about it. But as we set off again, I was painfully aware that yet again we'd lost valuable time. I checked my phone. Yep, 8:00 p.m. I'd be back in time for breakfast.

Elke had put in her mix CD and was murmuring along to "Into the Night" from *Twin Peaks*. The haunting music seemed to carry us farther into the forest.

"The perfect spooky music for being lost in the dark at night," Elke whispered.

"Cut it out, Elke." Natasha's fingers trembled a little on the steering wheel.

"Come on," said Elke. "This is the most excitement you've had your entire life!"

Oh, how I hated her. Like being ditched in a forest was fun. I should never have tried to get back at her.

"Can we just go home and never speak to each other again?" I raised my brows. "Please, pretty please?" How was I going to survive in the car with them for another eight hours? I had no idea. "Or maybe just take me to the freeway and I'll hitch a ride."

"Sounds good," said Natasha. She scowled at me. "Don't worry, we won't miss you."

I was about to snap back when another voice spoke up.

There is a faster route to your destination. Click Accept to follow new route.

Natasha's map app had come back to life.

12

NATASHA TAPPED ACCEPT. *IN ONE THOUSAND FEET, TURN left.*

"What are you doing? We know where we're going." Elke grabbed Natasha's phone.

Natasha slammed on the brakes. "Leave my app alone!"

Darius skidded to a stop just in time to keep from colliding with us. "For fuck's sake, Natasha." He banged on her window.

Natasha opened it and pointed to her app. "Faster route, we take the next left."

"And does it look like there's a left turn near here?" He didn't hide his irritation. I didn't blame him. There could be anything ahead. It was a narrow road climbing ever uphill, lined with tall trees on both sides.

He sighed. "Just follow this road. The faster we get away from here, the better. It's only a matter of time before all that lightning starts another fire. I don't want to be around for that." Darius stared up at the rust-stained sky.

Elke tapped her phone again. "Look, if we stay on this road like you said, it's almost like a U-turn. Do you really want to go back the way we came? We're just losing time."

Just then a light came up on the dashboard and Natasha sighed.

"Shit, is that the low gas light?" Darius asked.

"Yes, and why I'm following the app. And not listening to you." Natasha put the car into drive.

"Wait, I thought your Prius was electric!" I leaned forward to see the warning light for myself.

"No need to panic, Lily." Natasha tapped the light like that would stop it. "It's a hybrid. They run on gas, but get way better mileage."

"It should have at least thirty miles left," said Elke like she knew everything about gas and mileage and warning systems. "We'll be fine as long as we don't get lost."

"Yes," Darius agreed. "We keep going on the roads I know, so you make it safely to the freeway."

Elke looked from Natasha to Darius. "I side with Darius."

"You would. He's your girlfriend's brother." Natasha said it like an insult, and the way she glared at Darius made it seem as if her anger was aimed at him.

I watched Elke to see if she saw that too, but she just looked confused. Darius wasn't all about taking *us* to safety; he was all about taking Natasha.

"If we're voting, I vote with Natasha," I said. "Following the app makes more sense. If it saves time, it saves gas." I was not voting for Natasha, only for getting out of there.

"It's too risky." Elke crossed her arms.

82

"That's the way I'm going. If you don't like it, you can get a ride with Darius. I'm sure he won't mind." Natasha was queen of the sarcastic smiles.

Darius shook his head. "There's no way I'm leaving you out here." When Natasha loudly ignored him, he addressed Elke. "Can you imagine Sasha's reaction if I left you behind?"

"Too right, and you'd deserve it!" Elke sighed and strapped back up. "Okay, we follow the stinking app."

We set off again, slower, to make sure we didn't miss the left turn, or the "mythical turn" as Elke called it.

My phone vibrated. Shit, I'd missed a call from Mom when my phone was out of range. The call had gone to voicemail. I tried to listen discreetly.

Hi, Lily, this is Mom. I know you've been waiting for the results as much as me, and while they're not…what we hoped for…

"Wait, what?" That was it? The call must have dropped.

"Okay back there, Lily?" Of course, Natasha would have noticed my dismay.

"Yep, everything's fine," I muttered. So not fine. "Not what we hoped for"… What does that even mean? She's still sick, worse than before? Oh my God. Oh my God. I called back. But it wouldn't connect. I tried again and again.

Thunder crashed overhead, and lightning split across the sky. But it all seemed unreal. How could I still be here when Mom was going through that alone?

"Would you rather?" Elke started.

"Seriously?" Natasha cut Elke dead. And for once I was thankful.

Elke didn't even reply. She just crossed her legs and sat in stony silence.

I pulled my hoodie on. The wind blew against the car, pushing us from side to side.

In fifty feet, turn left. Turn left. Go straight ahead then.

"Crap." Natasha slowed down. "We missed it."

We all looked around. There was no left turn. Only the outline of trees and Darius's headlamps cutting through the dim light.

"You didn't miss it. It wasn't there." Elke was so smug.

The tension was like the air before a summer thunderstorm, heavy and bristling with electricity. There was no way we were all going to survive in this car together.

Elke fiddled with her phone. "Screw this, no signal again." She frowned at Darius's headlights shining in the side-view mirror. "What are you doing to him? He's following you around like a lost dog. What's going on between you two, anyway?"

"Nothing." Natasha rolled her eyes.

"Nothing? Come on, you can't fool me." Elke nudged Natasha's arm.

Natasha sighed. "We had a thing, but I ended it."

"Wow, what, you've been *dating*? I thought you were just good friends. No wonder he was pissed! You dumped him and still expected him to play the douchebag role for us? He must love you! Does Sasha know?" Elke got out her phone, ready to text Sasha. "Oh, shoot. I forgot. No signal. But seriously, we could have all hung out together."

"And that is why I didn't tell you."

"Nice. That's why you didn't come and find me, too busy with each other. Good to know where your loyalties lie." Elke shook her head. "He adores you; that's obvious. Why else follow us into hell?"

"It's not hell. It's the right way out of here. Anyway, now that he's at UC Davis, we don't need to be long-distance dating during his freshmen year. It's distracting." It sounded like she'd practiced those lines over and over. Until she almost believed them. All those glances, the arguments, that pent-up tension, made sense now. It's easier to drop someone than to be dropped. I should know.

"Sounds like your sister talking, not you," Elke pointed out.

"She's still right. I've got a lot to focus on this year, without the distractions of a doomed romance." Natasha white-knuckled the steering wheel. One of her perfect nails was chipped.

We drove on in silence. Lightning cracked across the sky too fast for the thunder to catch up with it. The glowing smoke plume swirled higher, as if it was trying to reach out for us. Thank God, the actual fire was miles away. At least I hoped it was.

Elke pointed at it. "See that? We should be heading toward the smoke, not away from it, if we want to get around and back onto the freeway."

Little beads of sweat formed a line above Natasha's lips. "The app said the road was just here. It's mountainous. It can't go in straight north-south lines."

Lightning forked across the valley. Then again. Followed by a crash of thunder.

"Look, look! Left turn!" I practically squealed.

Natasha swung the car down the road and beamed at me. "Nice

catch, Lily!" And yes, it did make my heart glow. Darius's motorcycle screeched as it made the sudden turn.

It was a narrow road, but it was a road. No fire road gate to pass through, no fire warning or road closure signs, and best of all it was headed toward the fire. Just like Elke said it should be. We bumped on through a little meadow, past a collapsed-looking red barn, and on into sparsely spaced trees that rapidly crowded together to become a forest. We drove along a tunnel of branches, but not being able to see all that smoke made it feel better, like we were actually getting somewhere. Except there was no way to know for sure.

I asked Natasha. "How is the gas lasting?"

She shrugged.

"We can't have gone more than ten miles. That gives us at least twenty miles of gas left. The freeway can't be more than three from here," Elke said. "At least according to TRX. We can keep track of the odometer, count down the miles left of gas." She frowned. "Does that even make sense?"

Not really, but neither did her judgment of how much gas was left.

"The odometer reads one hundred and thirty thousand miles." A little line formed between Natasha's eyes as she double-checked. She saw me watching in the mirror and frowned. "Yes, exactly that."

"So, it's a countdown. Let us know every mile we pass," Elke ordered.

Thunder echoed above us but less frequently, and the lightning had moved off into the distance. I almost missed the flashes. At least they helped light up the forest. The car headlights only highlighted how dark it was around us as we continued deeper into the unknown.

I checked my phone: still no new messages or texts. What did she mean, not the good news we were expecting? Was she worried about me worrying about her? It couldn't be the worst. It just couldn't. My nails dug into my palms as I clenched my fists without realizing. Deep breaths. I coughed. The air was getting smokier, so we had to be going the right way.

Natasha shuddered. "This is so creepy. It doesn't even feel like a road."

The car bounced and swerved a little. Natasha slapped Elke's hand away from the CD. "Leave it. I want to hear what's going on." She wound down her window.

"Why don't you stop and ask Darius what he thinks?" I suggested.

Natasha cut me down. "I already know what he thinks."

He revved the motorcycle impatiently behind us.

Natasha sped up, then slowed back down. The ground was dry enough to make the car skid. An owl hooted in the dark and a screechy sound followed.

"What is that?" Elke asked. "It sounds lonely and scared."

"A fox maybe?" I suggested.

"Will you both just shut up and let me focus," Natasha snapped.

Elke and I sat in silence for the next mile.

I coughed. The smell of smoky haze filled the car. "Can you close the window again?" I'd be so glad when fire season was over.

Natasha rolled it back up. "One."

"What?" I asked.

"One mile, done."

"Would you rather—"

"No," said Natasha, before Elke could say anything else.

"Have you got any more water?" It came out like a whimper. "Please?"

"There's a spare can in the back. But I'm not stopping until we hit the freeway."

"Okay, no problem." I shared wide eyes with Elke.

"Here, have some of mine." Elke passed me hers.

I drank the last few sips, wiped my mouth, and smiled. "Thanks."

She nodded and turned back to face the front.

It was stifling. I could hardly breathe. There was no air.

"Stop. I'm going to be sick." I clutched my chest.

Natasha stopped.

I swung open the door and instantly felt better. I blinked to get the itching feeling of smoke from my eyes. "False alarm." I closed the door.

"Ready now? I knew you'd be a nightmare to travel with." Natasha rolled her eyes.

I glared at her. "Thanks for your concern. It wasn't exactly my first choice either."

"Yet here you are," Natasha snapped back. "No one made you come on this trip. You make it sound like you had no choice but to be here, like this whole situation is my fault, or Elke's, but never yours."

"If I'd known we were going to have a five-hour detour where you dumped me in the forest, I wouldn't have come!" I said.

"It's not like you're blameless. You tried to lose me in the forest," Elke said. "You're the reason we're out here in the dark, instead of back on the freeway." So, Elke hadn't forgiven me.

"I didn't meticulously plan it like you and Natasha did with that fake crash. That was unreal. I was just getting a little payback. Wouldn't you?"

"Um, I seem to recall you started a panic at the Yosemite Adventure Camp that spread a fire and threw the blame on us!" Natasha lurched forward as the car bounced over a washboard in the road.

"It was your *fault*!" That came out so whiny. I swallowed and tried again. "I said sorry, and I am." I held myself tight and gazed at the back of Elke's head. "If we could have just talked about it instead of doing these stupid pranks, we would be almost home now."

Natasha narrowed her eyes. "Too late now."

She slowed the car down even more. The wind buffeted the branches, scraping them across the roof as we drove by.

"If you must know, I was going to tell you that the car was full already, but my mom forced me to take you because of your poor, sad family situation. I didn't tell her what a bitch you were. So, there's that." Natasha pursed her lips.

I was so over this conversation. "Okay. What's done is done. It's history. Let's just get out of here. We don't have to be friends or speak to each other ever again." I had bigger things to worry about.

"Thank God for that." Natasha raised an eyebrow at me. But her voice had softened.

"It was a stupid prank," said Elke, "especially on a night like this with a lightning storm. And if we hadn't done that, you wouldn't have paid me back, and we wouldn't be lost right now." She flashed a look at Natasha that I couldn't quite make out. But at least things were less tense now.

"I thought you liked being lost in the dark." I gave her a quick smile. "It's okay. No one got hurt, and we're all still here, right?" Jesus, I couldn't wait to get away from them. "It's an adventure I would never have had without you. Something to write about in my college app. I won't use your actual names." I said it like this was all such a laugh. I was scowling inside, but I wasn't going to show it.

Natasha sighed. "I just want to get out of here." Her voice shook a little. There were deep shadows under her eyes. She was probably as exhausted and stressed as I was. None of us wanted to be in that car.

The Prius finally slowed all the way down to a crawl and then a stop.

Darius came to a slow stop behind us. He yelled out, "What's up?"

Elke leaned over to check the odometer. "We've easy got ten miles left in there. Only two miles to go."

"I think there's something in the road. Pass me your phone!" Natasha shone the flashlight on the road ahead.

A deep crack ran across the road, but worse than that was the huge pile of logs stacked ten feet behind it. Our route to the freeway was blocked.

13

"WHAT THE HELL?" DARIUS JUMPED OFF HIS MOTORCY-cle and ran toward the log pile. "What is that doing there?" He pushed it, as if an eight-foot-high log pile would just roll out of his way.

"Trust the app?" Elke scorned. She got out the car, slamming the door behind her. If anger was an energy, she'd be able to move the logs by herself. "Don't just sit there." She stomped over to join Darius.

I exchanged a look with Natasha. Her face was pinched and hollow. All that on-our-way-home energy had vanished in an instant.

"We should go and help." The car door creaked as I pushed it, ready to get out. It swung right back onto my shins. Perfect, I'd have a memento bruise, like I'd ever forget tonight. I pushed the door back open.

Natasha slumped her head down on the steering wheel, hiding it in her arms. I reached out to put my hand on her shoulder but hesitated. There was something about her silence, a force field around her. As if she was holding everything tightly together, waiting for me to leave so she could break down. Alone.

"Are you okay?" I whispered, which was a stupid question. Obviously she wasn't.

"Go," she inhaled sharply. Her throat was thick with tears.

I clambered out and joined Elke and Darius at the foot of the log mound. There was dirt in between the logs and weeds. They must have been there a while. They were piled up haphazardly, like a giant Jenga pile. The ones at the top looked like they could just roll off and crush us, and the ones at the base were never going to move.

"Got a forklift?" I joked to Elke.

Darius shook his head. "We're never going to get through here, and there's no guarantee we're even on the right road following Natasha's app. I knew it. I should have pushed harder, convinced her I was right."

"Good luck with that." Elke kicked the pile. "You know how Natasha is once she gets an idea in her head…no backing down."

"We have to get through. We can't go back. We don't have enough gas." The panic rose in my voice.

"Thanks for the reminder." Elke glanced at Darius. "I don't know if there's enough to get us to the gas station, to be honest."

"Not easily another twenty miles of gas left then?" I knew she was just trying to reassure Natasha. But that's not much help when reality confronts you with the brutal truth. "So, we are stuck out here?" I don't know why I even asked.

Elke didn't even bother to answer. She just got ready to push, hands on the logs, feet planted firmly.

"Okay," said Darius, "let's do it."

I joined in, pushing forward with all my weight. It was hot and hard work, and the pile didn't budge at all. My feet slipped on the dry earth, and even when we turned to put our backs into it, all I got were scrapes from the logs.

Thunder growled above us. Lightning flashed, cracking open the sky like an eggshell. "I've never seen so much lightning." I couldn't stop flinching at every boom and crack.

Darius breathed heavily as he took a break from pushing.

Elke gazed at the sky. "Would you rather be struck by lightning or consumed by fire?" She raised her eyebrows.

"Neither." Jesus. I shoved myself at a log and bounced off. "It's hopeless."

Elke thrust her whole body against the pile, her Doc Marten boots slipped in the dry soil, and sweat poured off her face. This was never going to work. She glared at the car. "What the hell is Natasha doing in there, anyway?"

"She just needs a moment," said Darius.

I could see her shoulders heaving in the dusk light. Elke didn't even turn to look.

"Okay, but now we all know not to trust her stupid app." Elke kicked the log pile. It shifted and the top one trembled. "See, we can move them! Come on, try harder!"

We pushed on the top log together. Then the one next to it. Then the one by the side of that. They might as well have been cemented into place. The dirt between them shifted a little, falling like sand, but the logs had stuck themselves firmly together. A bug scurried out and ran along my arm. I flicked it off in disgust before I could even see what it was.

"It's only a millipede." Elke had a smudge of mud on her nose, and her violet hair stuck to the sweat on her cheeks.

There was no way we were going to move this pile, no matter how much effort we put into it.

Elke kicked the pile again, then hopped around on one foot. "It's only a mile away. We should climb over and walk."

"Yeah, right," said Darius. "In the dark, not knowing if we're even walking the right way, through a forest full of dried fuel and lightning bolts hitting all around. Smart choice."

"But it's so close. We have to try," Elke pleaded.

I stood there blinking as my insides twisted. She could not be serious.

"We don't even know if the road continues beyond that pile. I'll go and get gas from the station. You stay here in the car. When I get back, you follow me out the way we should have gone. At least get to the freeway and check in at a motel. There's no way Natasha can drive all the way home now, anyway." Darius picked up his helmet.

My heart sank, but I knew he was right. At least I could call Mom from a motel. She was probably waiting for me to call back to find out her news. The news that wasn't what we were hoping for. I shivered and pushed my fear away. First, we needed to get out of here.

"That nearest gas station was out of gas, remember? You sure you want to go running around finding a gas station that still has gas and is open, instead of helping us move the logs?" Elke wasn't giving up so fast.

"I'm not leaving you stranded out here. It might take a little longer, but I'll be back with gas. I promise." Darius walked back to the car and tapped on Natasha's window.

94

She opened it and they talked in hushed voices. By her tight mouth and narrowed eyes, she didn't look pleased, but she nodded and wiped her eyes, and then Darius leaned in and kissed her. I turned away to give them some privacy.

"Don't worry, we'll get out of here." Elke spat on the ground. "What is it with you two? You got a death wish or something?"

"What?" I was so startled by the question that I fell back onto the logs.

"You, siding with Natasha back there, after the way she's treated you. If you'd sided with me and Darius, we'd be back on the freeway by now."

"You don't know that." My sinking heart knew she was right. Oh God. I looked up to the dark sky. Were we ever leaving this hellhole? "Darius could have been wrong. We could have still been as lost."

"Yes, but not down a dead-end road with almost no gas." Elke smiled tightly. "Shit, I'm sorry. It's all getting to me."

"I know the feeling."

We walked back to the Prius. Elke and I waved goodbye to Darius after Natasha hugged him like she'd never see him again.

"Made up then?" Elke asked as Darius disappeared down the road.

"Yes," and Natasha smiled as she hugged herself.

We sat in the Prius waiting for Darius to get back, watching the light change from damson twilight to a darker burnt sienna. A hawk flew off into the smoky night from a nearby tree, squawking as it went.

I tutted and recrossed my legs, knocking the Oak Canyon folder out of my bag. I stuffed it back in. I could kiss that dream goodbye if Mom's news was the worst. She'd need all the support she could get. My heart ripped a little.

"A mile away," Elke repeated like I hadn't heard her the first time. "I can't believe we're just going to sit in here and wait for Darius forever when I could be at the freeway by now."

"Walking in the dark to who knows where!" I answered. I couldn't believe she still thought it was a good idea. She was as stubborn as Natasha.

Elke shook her head. "I'm going in anyway."

"But you can't, not alone." I waited for her to agree or persuade me to go with her. But she didn't.

"She's right." At first, I thought Natasha was siding with Elke. "We should wait for Darius to get back. The last thing he needs is to find us gone and have to rescue us from being lost in the woods again, or worse. Who knows what's beyond the log pile." And then I realized she was all about supporting Darius. "Maybe it was out there to stop you from driving into a canyon."

"A canyon?" Elke sneered. "Your precious app said it was a road. Don't you believe it anymore?" She rolled her eyes in disgust.

"I think we should stay here and wait," I said softly.

"Seriously? You're chickening out again?" Elke glared at me. "You always do whatever Natasha wants."

Talk about irony. "Um, that would be you."

Elke gave me a WTF frown.

"I didn't realize I was so popular," said Natasha. She did, though, and she loved it. "We are not climbing over that horror pile into the unknown when Darius is coming back with gas to get us out of here. Anyway, you said the app was stupid." Natasha raised her brows.

"What if I'm wrong, and it's our best shot? Obviously, it didn't know about this stupid log pile. But we can climb over. Or I can go alone, and you can wait for Darius," Elke offered.

This was going nowhere fast. "It's dark. Any of these lightning strikes could start another fire." A streak zigzagged across the sky followed by a roll of thunder, followed by another streak. Every time the sky lit up, it showed how deep in the forest we were. "The car is the safest place."

"For how long?" Elke scowled. "All night? Until someone else finds it burned out and surrounded by fire?"

Natasha sighed. "You're so dramatic. The forest fire isn't anywhere near here."

"Yet," said Elke.

NIGHT

14

THE WIND SHOOK AGAINST THE CAR AND SENT LEAVES swirling over the hood. We sat there silently, listening for Darius's return. Every crack of lightning and rumble of thunder had me twitching, but the thunder had gone from a rumble to a murmur, and the lightning had finished its final flash across the sky and disappeared over the mountains to the south. It was beating us home.

"Oh my God." Elke combed her hands through her hair. "It's been forty minutes. Are we going to wait all night for him to show up?"

"Give him a chance. He'll be back."

"Right, and meanwhile we could have made it to the freeway by now." Elke stretched her neck from side to side. "What do you say, Lily?"

"Darius can't be much longer. There must be at least one gas station with gas around here. We can get back to that diner, back to civilization, and figure out the route from there." I suggested.

"She's right," Natasha agreed. "He'll be back any minute now. And then we can all get out of here, together."

"Together? You weren't so bothered about that before." Elke glanced at Natasha. "For either me or Lily."

"Oh, let it go already! It's not like I was ever going to leave you, or her." Natasha glared at me as if I was the one needling her.

"They mentioned the storm on the radio. You knew it was coming and went ahead with the prank anyway." I took a deep breath. "I don't know what I ever saw in you." My best friend. A long time ago. "Guess I know better now, too."

"Huh. You pranked back, knowing about the storm." Natasha shook her head in amazement. "You know nothing. You ruined everything!"

"It was eighth grade! You were my best friend." It was true, so she might as well know. It wasn't like we'd ever be close again. Sleepovers, whispering past midnight, sharing our first crushes, that wasn't real to her?

"You know what I think? We're all a little emotional, and we should save all that for another time." Elke raised her brows at me. "You okay?"

I nodded. No, I was not fucking okay. Natasha had rewritten my childhood. My mom could be dying, and we were all stuck together in this stupid car.

"Okay, I'm going to set a timer. It's nine fifteen, if Darius isn't back by nine twenty-five, I'm making a break for the freeway. Who's in?" Elke clasped her hands together, looking from Natasha to me and back to Natasha again.

I nodded. "Okay." At least the storm had moved on.

Natasha shook her head. "It's too dangerous, Elke. You know that."

"No risk, no reward," Elke replied with a grin.

Every minute felt like an hour. And every time I looked up, the outside seemed darker. "Do you think we should have the interior lights off?" I asked. "So we don't get a dead battery?" Anyone outside could see us lit up like a beacon in the dark. A moth collided with the windshield.

"Good idea," said Elke, turning off the lights and plunging us into darkness.

"Shit, Elke!" Natasha exclaimed.

"Calm down. Your eyes will get used to it in a few moments," Elke said.

"What's that—more of your 'dropping' training?" Natasha answered sarcastically.

Elke opened her door and swung her legs out. "I'm going to find the freeway. Come with me or stay there. Just don't kill each other in my absence." She pointed her phone flashlight at the pile of logs. "Coming?"

I stayed firmly in my seat. There was no point rushing off before waiting out the time we'd agreed on.

"There's still two minutes." Natasha shook her head. "Wait."

"What for? He's not coming back." Elke walked to the log pile, grinned like she was performing for us, and clambered over it. There was a clatter as a log fell when she reached the top, and a crash as it landed. Then Elke disappeared from sight.

"I'm okay," Elke yelled back. "See you later, suckers." Her phone light quickly evaporated into the surrounding darkness.

"We should go after her," I said. "Anything could happen."

Natasha rolled her eyes. "You just literally chose not to. Anyway, it's Elke. Nothing hurts her. She'll find the freeway and get a ride home."

"Why aren't you going after her then?" I asked.

"Because it's not the smart thing to do. Elke will survive, but I'm not so sure about me."

I got out. The storm might have moved on, but the wind still whipped around the treetops.

"I'm not letting Elke go alone."

Natasha opened the car door. "You tried to get her lost earlier, and now you want to save her?"

I waited while Natasha huffed and looked in the direction of where Elke had disappeared. She fiddled with the car keys in her hand. "Come on, you're not seriously thinking of following her. You said we should stick together."

"Exactly. We can't leave her. Anything could happen."

"Anything could happen to us chasing after her," Natasha replied.

"So, you're scared, that's all. And I thought you were besties."

"Of course I'm scared. I'd be an idiot not to be."

We looked at the log pile. "I am, too. But I'll never forgive myself if I don't go after her."

"It was her choice. It's Elke. She'll be fine." Natasha's voice wobbled a touch.

"Are you sure?"

Natasha swept the hair from her face. "Okay, you win. But you don't even like her."

"I don't *not* like her. What happened was a long time ago. We're different people now." Though to be honest, I was not sure anymore who Natasha was then or now.

"Okay, let's go." She got out the car and slammed the door behind her. "Seriously, Elke will be the death of me." She said it like a joke, but it gave me the chills.

We forced our way through the shrubs and ferns around the edge of the log pile. It was thick with vegetation; my phone light barely lit the way. It was so like Elke to climb over all dramatically when she could have just gone around.

There wasn't a road after the logs. There was a ditch. A giant crack had opened up, probably from the drought. We were lucky not to trip into it. I hoped Elke had managed to avoid it, too. After that was a narrow trail, partially covered in foliage. The logs had been piled up as a safety measure—don't go here, it doesn't lead anywhere. And Elke had stubbornly forced her way past it anyway. Natasha and I walked on—stumbled, to be more precise—heads bowed against the low branches, feet tentatively finding their way past fern clumps, rocks, and roots.

An owl hooted far away, a great horned owl, I think. I wondered what other creatures were hiding in here, watching as we passed.

"What?" asked Natasha. "What can you see?" She looked where I was looking up at the tree canopy. A bat darted out and around and swooped out of sight. "God, I hate the outdoors."

"Seriously? I thought because Elke loved it, you must, too. That whole Yosemite Adventure Camp… Why did you go if you don't like the outdoors?"

"Same reason as you. To be with Elke."

"No." I did not want to be with Elke. "I hated her back then." A caterpillar rolled around in my stomach.

Natasha nodded her head, and an annoying smile played on her face. "Love and hate, two sides of the same coin. Come on, admit it, you loved her just like everyone else!"

"I did not. Shit." I stubbed my toe on a rock. "That's ridiculous."

"Whatever." Natasha pushed ahead. "Ugh, I just stepped in something."

I focused by flashlight on a pile of freshly dug-up soil. "Ants' nest?"

Natasha brushed off her legs. "Nope, no ants."

"Bear poo?"

Natasha shuddered. "I hope not. Let's keep moving. I can't believe she got this far in five minutes."

We were trying to stick to the trail, but it felt more like the trail was closing in on itself. Shrubs and branches rustled as they moved to block our way. I knew it was really the wind, which had picked up since Elke's departure.

I huddled in my hoodie. "I never thought I might actually get cold."

"I didn't think I'd actually be leaving the car, apart from getting gas and peeing." Natasha checked under her boots again. "I think that was poop. Never mind. Let's call out. She couldn't have gotten much farther."

I nodded, and yelled, "Elke! Elke!"

Natasha tried, then I tried again. Nothing.

"Wait," Natasha held out her hand to stop me from walking. "What if she left the path?"

"Then she could be anywhere." Shit, I wish I'd ignored Natasha and left with Elke. Scratch that, I wish I'd never accepted the stupid ride, but it was too late, and here we were, enemies forever joined in our quest to find the one who had split us apart. Or had she?

"Elke?" I stopped to listen. The wind gusted through the leaves, a bird chirped out one croaked note, like an alarm call, and somewhere very far away a dog barked.

"What if we don't find her?"

"Of course, we'll find her." I snapped. "Sorry," I said as soon as I saw Natasha's crestfallen face. "I don't know. Let's not think about it."

"What if Elke is lost, and Darius is lost, and we're lost, and no one finds any of us, and we end up like those flyers of missing people?" Natasha's face was pale. She looked like she might puke.

"It's okay, we're together," I reassured her, even though it sounded like an oxymoron. I looked behind me. I was pretty sure I could find my way back, and if I could, Elke definitely could with her outdoorsy skills. "We're all going to be fine."

"Yeah, right, 'fine' like in a horror movie where only one girl survives, always the 'good white' girl," Natasha added.

"Not this time. This time, we all get out." Why did I even care about her? Natasha had already shown she didn't care about me. I glanced at her, hair knotted, dress ripped. She was fraying, and I felt for her. Somewhere under all that veneer, she was still Natasha, twelve-year-old Lily's best friend.

"You okay?" Natasha stopped to wait for me.

I nodded.

"I was a bit much earlier. I just get..." Natasha looked at the heavy night sky. "It's easier to hurt people than to be hurt, you know?" Was that an apology?

"We're all stressed. It's okay." I didn't care anymore, anyway. If I said that enough times, it would become true.

"Right." Natasha took a deep breath and yelled, "ELKE! ELKE!"

There was a scrabbling noise, and for a moment I expected a deer, or a fox, or even a bear to come out of the thicket, but it was Elke.

"Thank fuck, you finally came!" She grinned at us like we'd been playing a game. And I wondered if to her, we had been.

"Would you rather disappear alone, or with two friends?" I asked.

15

ELKE HADN'T FOUND THE FREEWAY, OR EVEN THE REST of the road. Instead, she'd been listening for clues, making nicks on tree trunks so she'd recognize if she'd gone back on herself, and hoping it wouldn't take too long for us to "get up from our lazy asses," and find her.

"If I'd known we'd be in this situation, I would have packed a flare gun," Elke assured us.

"Yep, but then you could have set off a fire, and that would have been really bad," I said.

"So, being lost in the woods, isn't?" Natasha asked.

"Better than being lost in the woods with a wildfire spreading." My skin crawled as the memory of the campfire night flashed in my head. The flickering flames racing across the parched ground. The tree exploding. I shook my head. I couldn't go back there, not ever. I looked up. Natasha and Elke hadn't even heard me.

"I can't believe it took you so long to find me." Elke looked accusingly at Natasha.

"I can't believe you left me." Natasha shot back.

They glared at each other in full face-off mode. At least I was out of it for now.

Natasha's hurt reminded me of all the times I'd backed down when she insisted we do something "exciting," and I hadn't wanted to. It started with candy, moved on to makeup, and ended with clothes—shoplifting, or as Natasha called it, sneaking things out. If I ever refused, I'd get sad Natasha, all pouts and despair, and instantly give in.

"I was busy saving your ass, like always." Elke snapped me out of my daze. "'Go save Lily, make my stupid plan work.'" So, it was Natasha's plan.

"If you'd found the freeway, you'd have left us!" Natasha yelled back at her.

Wow, that escalated fast.

"Us? Are you and Lily tight now?" Elke asked.

I glanced awkwardly at Natasha. We were in no way tight.

"No, I didn't think so," Elke continued. "I don't know what's going on with you, Natasha. I want my friend back. You know...the sweet, fun one? Not the boy-obsessed scaredy-cat."

I felt like I was watching a tennis match and about to be hit by the ball.

"Are you for real?" asked Natasha. "I only came to save you from yourself."

Elke cocked her chin. "I'm amazed you even came all the way out here. I mean, let's face it, there's no way you're making your own path. You're just going to follow your sister to college because you always do whatever you're told. Maybe that's why you turn the power play on your friends. 'Let's steal this nail polish. It will be so fun!' 'Oh wait, Elke, I'm scared. *You* hold the bag.' Story of your life, Natasha."

"Perhaps it's better than being in a hedonistic rush to the next excitement no matter what carnage you leave behind," Natasha snapped back.

I bit my lip. So, Natasha used Elke the same way she used me, shoplifting for kicks, without ever placing herself at risk. And we were too dumb to say no.

"It was your idea!" Elke screamed at Natasha.

"Like you don't care that Lily screwed up your life?" Natasha's eyes flashed.

"Yes, but not as much as you, it seems." Elke took a deep breath, then spoke very softly. "She didn't screw it up anyway. My life changed when my dad died, and it's not like she was responsible for that." The last word came out in a whisper.

There was a moment of silence. Then Natasha rushed to hug her. "I'm so sorry. I never meant... I take it all back. I don't know why we're even arguing." Tears rolled down her cheeks.

Elke hugged her back. "Me neither. Let's just get out of here."

Natasha nodded and they walked off together. Like I wasn't even there.

"So, which way now?" I called after them. Why did I ever think this would work? Even when we were lost, three was the loneliest number. Someone always gets pushed out. Me. It was always me.

"Hey, you." Elke waited for me to reach her. "Don't worry. It's done. I'm over it, and if I am, she has to be."

I liked Elke's direct way of talking and thinking, no games, no second-guessing. She just told it the way it was. I gave a her a grateful smile.

"That doesn't make us friends," she reminded me.

Obviously. I nodded.

"I've already tried this way." Elke pointed ahead. "It goes to a dried-up creek, so the freeway isn't that way, but it has to be close. Are you both with me on finding it, or are you going back to the car and waiting on Darius to save your asses?"

Natasha raised her brows at me, waiting for my reply.

Waiting for Darius was the obvious choice, but for how long? And there was something about Elke's supreme confidence. "Why don't we climb higher, see if we can look down on the freeway?" I suggested.

"Great idea," Elke replied. "This way it is then." She led the way, following a wiggly path uphill that must have once been a stream. It wouldn't be that much higher, but hopefully high enough to get a broader view.

We leaned into the slope, using our hands to steady us whenever if felt like we were slipping. The pine trees went so perfectly up hill, each slightly taller than the next, that they looked like they'd been combed into place. So different from the tangle of trunks and branches I'd got lost in earlier.

If a person disappears in the woods, were they ever really there? I shuddered.

I checked my phone again. Still no way to call Mom back. Anyway, what would I say? Lost, don't know where we are, or how we're getting back? It would hardly reduce her stress. The low power warning flashed. I stuffed the phone back in my pocket. And followed closer to Elke's flashlight. It wasn't like I had any signal anyway.

We picked up the pace. I stumbled, caught myself, and ran to catch up. My mouth was dry, and my stomach grumbled so loudly that I actually thought it was thunder.

"We should have brought water with us," Natasha said in between pants.

"Not long now," Elke assured her.

Elke and Natasha's footsteps crunched softly. They leaned toward each other like sisters, or best friends. What was I even doing here? Every time they patched things up, I was left alone again. At least I'd never have to see them after tonight. I'd be happy to ignore Natasha for the rest of my life. As far as I was concerned, she was just one more reason to get away from San Ramon.

But could I do that if Mom's results were bad? *Not what we were hoping for.* My chest hollowed. I held my breath, waiting for the wave of fear to pass.

I couldn't go away to college. I couldn't leave Mom alone to deal with whatever happened next. I'd go to community college. It was the only viable solution.

I looked up to see them both waiting for me. Arms crossed.

"Sorry, lost in thought," I mumbled.

A draft of wind rushed through the trees, shivering their branches, and far off a barn owl screeched.

"Screw this. Let's get back to the car," said Natasha. "Darius will probably be there wondering why we left."

"Let's just get to the top and take a look, because what if the freeway is only five minutes away?" Elke looked at me like I was the decider.

"We need to get the hell out of here," said Natasha. "It's so dark. It feels dangerous!"

She was right about that. Something about being there in the dark, with the creaking branches and the giant, gangly, limbs of lichen-covered trees, made the whole forest seem like a stage set for a movie where anything could happen. I'd be so happy to see the freeway. Right then, a ten-hour drive along the same long, boring road sounded like heaven.

"Let's toss a coin. Heads we go back, tails we go on to the summit," Elke suggested.

"I'm not choosing our route by chance." Natasha frowned. "It's foolish to keep going."

"Life is a game of chance," said Elke. She pulled out a quarter from her pocket. "Ready?"

Natasha nodded.

"I guess I have no choice," I said.

"Ta-da!" Elke revealed the coin and flipped it. "Tails," she said and smiled. "On to the summit."

Natasha rolled her eyes but obeyed. And I was hardly going to stay there alone. We trudged on upward.

"Weird how it feels almost normal now," said Elke. "No streetlights, no other cars, we could be on the people left in the world and we wouldn't know."

"You sure you didn't eat all your weed doughnut back there?" Natasha asked. "Please tell me we're going the right way."

"I think so," said Elke. "Isn't it amazing how fast your eyes adjust?"

She was right. I could see a lot better now, although what I was seeing wasn't all that reassuring, just trees and shrubs and ferns and the slope of the earth and the occasional rock and then, "Hey, that's a path!" I was so excited, I ran-fell into it.

It went from a small trail out into a rocky path, climbing steeply upward. I clutched onto bushes and ferns as I walked, just in case. I couldn't even see if I'd fall down a cliff or into a tree if I slipped.

"We're almost there. I can feel it." The hope in Elke's voice was infectious!

Puffs of wind swept through the trees, bringing the strong scent of smoke. I guess they were still battling that fire.

"Smell that smoke. Isn't it stronger than before?" Natasha obviously had the same worry.

"It is, but we're higher up so it has a clearer path to us." Elke sounded convincing, but I wasn't so sure. "It's okay. We'll be out of here soon, anyway," she reassured us.

"It's just smoke always makes me nervous, after almost getting evacuated last year." I gave a weak reassuring smile, like having to pack a to-go bag and find your pets, expecting to be evacuated any second, wasn't the slightest bit traumatic.

"I get it. It can move so fast, but trust me, that fire is miles away. We'll be long gone before it ever reaches this far." Elke smiled liked she knew, but she didn't. She'd left before fire seasons on the West Coast started getting really bad.

Natasha caught my eye. "It's not that close," she reassured me. "We'll be well away from here before it gets anywhere near us. Besides, the wind is going in the other direction."

"Hey, look!" Elke ran ahead and beamed back at us. "You were right, Lily. You were right!"

I scrambled up to her. Natasha followed closely behind. There it was, the top of the hill. The beautiful top, with a clear view across the valley. The smoke plume from the Wolf Hollow wildfire billowed across the sky. And below us in the valley were three smaller fires, glowing with orange intensity.

16

"SHIT, IT MUST HAVE BEEN THE LIGHTNING." ELKE LEANED over the top. "Still, they're small."

"At the moment." I looked down at them. "We should call it in."

"Right, on our no-signal phones." Natasha squinted at the fires. "They're at least a mile away, and it's not like they're that big."

"But we can see them," I added.

"They're not close enough to worry about." Elke looked at Natasha for confirmation.

"As long as the wind doesn't change." Natasha pulled Elke's sleeve. "Get back."

"Would you rather fall from a great height or sink into quicksand?" Elke asked, safely back from the edge.

"Quicksand," said Natasha. "I'd at least have a chance. You just lie on your back."

"And get sucked under," Elke finished.

"With a fall, there's no getting out of it." I turned around and grinned. Then I felt the crumbling ground I stood on give way.

My left foot slipped, and suddenly my legs were over the edge of the cliff. Scree clattered down the cliffside like falling marbles as I tried to gain a foothold. My breath came out in fast, sharp gulps. I leaned forward, trying to scrabble back up on my stomach. Why had I stood so close to the edge? I grabbed hold of a nearby shrub. It bent and snapped off. My right foot slipped.

"Help!"

Elke and Natasha rushed over to me. I reached up to Natasha, but she stepped back. She stepped back! My right foot slid further. I glanced down, big mistake. Nothing but rocks for a thousand feet and then pointy-tipped pines. If I didn't bounce to death, I'd be impaled.

My stomach clenched. "A little fucking help!"

"Here." Elke dropped down to lie on her stomach and held out her hand. "Grab hold of me."

My sweaty palm slipped. Elke grabbed it tighter with both hands. I found a foothold, then another, and finally scrambled back up. Jesus. I crawled away from the edge and sat shaking.

I could hardly find words. "You," I stammered at Natasha.

She rushed over to me. "Are you okay? Oh my God, that was so scary."

"That was so scary? You backed away when I needed you!"

"I did not." But she blushed and looked at her feet.

Elke nodded at Natasha. "I think you did."

Natasha tried again. "I'm sorry, I froze. I'm hopeless in a crisis." She tried to laugh it off. "I never meant for you to fall. You know that right?" She bit her lip. "I'm sorry. I don't know what happened."

Laughing it off as hopeless made it worse. What the hell was I doing there?

I stood and brushed myself off. "No freeway, that's for sure."

This was not a safe place to be—high up on the ledge watching the wildfires spread. Waiting for Darius back at the car was the only option. We didn't even need to discuss it.

We raced, half falling, half running, back along the tiny trail, thrashing angrily at anything in our path. Plants scratched my face and arms. Elke pushed back a branch and it smacked me in the stomach. I didn't care. I just wanted out of there.

What if I'd fallen and that was the end? Would Natasha even care? I swallowed. Now was not the time to overthink things. Just reach the tree ahead, then the ferns over there, and the next pine, and breathe. The sounds of bootsteps crunching through the undergrowth, the snap of twigs, and the wind gusting through the branches were my focus. I stared at the ground as it sloped downward. My calves were in rebellion as I tried to stop myself from speeding down out of control and landing on my rear. Natasha and Elke panted on either side of me, as determined not to speak as I was.

We reached the bottom, safely back in the woods, if that could be considered safe.

"Here." Elke pointed at a tree. "I marked it, so we can find the way back."

I nodded, too tired and pissed off to talk. Elke didn't say anything to Natasha. It was like she didn't think that was a terrible thing at all. The pair of them were awful. But at least Elke had grabbed my hand. I shivered. It felt like I was being watched again, but I didn't care. It wasn't like anything could be worse than what had already happened. I glared into the woods, daring whatever it was to come out and face me.

"Oh crap." Elke jumped over something ahead. "Look at that!" She pointed to a hunk of metal. "Rusty old trap. Did not expect to see that out here." She poked it with a stick. The metal jaws pinged closed, snapping the stick in half.

"Jesus, Elke, that could have taken your foot off." Natasha swung around. "What if there's more?" *Now* she was concerned.

"We should be more careful where we're walking." Elke shone her phone flashlight out among the trees, searching for another marked trunk.

"There's a broken branch there," Natasha pointed out. She walked over to it, careful to make sure there was nothing hidden in her way. She turned as if she was about to say something, took another step forward, and disappeared.

For a second, I was too shocked to move. Her scream told us she was alive. The echo, that she had plummeted below us, possibly into a cave.

Elke and I rushed to where Natasha had stood, stopping before that fateful extra step. I pushed the brush away to see where she'd fallen. There was a dark pit, about eight foot deep, covered with carefully placed branches, and layered with ferns—a crevasse that had been turned into a deliberate trap.

"Natasha?" Elke called down.

"Help!" Natasha's voice splintered, like it hurt to speak.

"Are you okay?" I asked.

"Of course, I'm not fucking okay!" Natasha yelled back. So, she *was* okay.

I raised my eyebrows at Elke. She ignored me and called down, "We're going to get you out of there."

"You better," Natasha yelled hesitantly, like she wasn't sure she believed us.

I so did not want to go down there.

Elke held out her hand. "Anything broken? Can you reach me and climb back up?"

"No," and this time Natasha actually whimpered. "I think I broke my ankle." She swayed a little like she was going to pass out.

"Okay. Sit down. Prop your leg up. We'll come to you." Elke shone her flashlight on Natasha. "I see you. It's going to be okay. Don't worry, we'll get you out of there."

"So, you keep saying," Natasha murmured.

We both looked down. A couple of twisted fir trees grew around the edges, their roots reaching for soil that wasn't there. Natasha had landed on a scrawny bush, which was probably why she wasn't more seriously hurt.

"Shit," Elke murmured and sat back on her heels.

"What are we going to do?" I whispered, as if Natasha would hear us.

"Why are you looking at me?" Elke huffed.

"You're supposed to be a survival expert!"

"What if I'm not?" Elke snapped.

"Maybe we can climb down, or send a rope down, a belt," I suggested. Like either of us had belts that long or were wearing belts at all.

I paced around the edge while Elke stared into the crevasse.

"Elke, Lily?" Natasha called up. "You still there?"

Did she think we'd forgotten her? "We're figuring out how to get you out." I shimmied over on my tummy so she could see me. "Can you stretch up and reach my hands?" I waggled them down as far as I could.

Natasha hobbled over, wincing with every step, and reached up. The tips of our fingers didn't quite touch.

"Maybe Elke can hold onto your legs, and you can reach down further?"

"And then what happens when you pull her in?" Elke asked, coming up behind me.

"There's a sort of slope." She pointed to a mound on the far side. It looked like the roof had caved in a little more. A crevasse of crumbling, moving dry earth was not a good place to be. "You can get along if you're careful. It shouldn't be too hard." Natasha sat in the middle staring up at us, all eyes and hope.

I glanced at Elke. "Are we really doing this?"

"With no phones, in the middle of nowhere? It's the only option. If we can get down, we can get up."

"True." Was it though, or was it like an arrow going in that can only come back out by tearing through the flesh?

"I know she left you in the woods, took ages to come after me, and didn't exactly rush to help when you slipped, but once upon a time, she was your best friend. There must be a reason we both loved her, right? And even if you don't buy into that, tough because I'm going down."

"Okay, let's do it." I don't know why I agreed. It would have made more sense for one of us to go back to the car in case Darius was there. He could ride off for help. But I was tired, scared, hurt, and over everything.

Elke was right. I did love Natasha years ago. I would have done anything for her. I did in fact do the most terrible thing for her, in my own way. "If we enter there, slowly, carefully"—I pointed to the dirt mound at the far end—"I think we might be able to inch down."

"On our butts?" Elke grinned.

"Yep, on our butts." It made more sense to go that way. The slope wasn't that bad, and it was better to see ahead than to try to go down backward. And this way we could see Natasha waving us on.

I inched my way down, wishing my jeans were thicker. Looking back up at where we'd come from was like looking up from a well. Surrounded by dark, earth walls, above us a patch of sky covered by a shroud of thick cloud, below our feet, dirt, rocks, roots, and occasional bones. Small ones, animal ones, I was sure. But it still made me shudder.

A star appeared as the clouds separated overhead, a reminder that the universe was so much bigger than three lost girls. The clouds gathered again, making the sky almost as dark as the pit.

Elke came down much faster, right after me. We were all back together, but no closer to getting home.

"So how do we get out? My leg is killing me." Natasha's voice trembled. She was in more pain than I'd realized.

"Let's take your boot off." Elke sat down on the dirt next to Natasha. "See if you can move your foot."

"Nope," Natasha shook her head. "It feels like the boot is the only thing holding it in place. I'm not trusting you to put it back together. Find me a stick, and I'll hobble out."

"Yes, ma'am." Elke started looking for one.

I did too, shining my fading phone flashlight into the dark corners. It was a weird space. Whoever made the trap had dug out a crevasse that already existed. One side was gnarled and full of roots and ivy; the other was smoother and still had the sharp indents of a shovel. Before the temporary roof had been attached, light would have filtered down, hence the feeble bush that Natasha had landed on, now broken in the middle. The crevasse was long and narrow. Stretched out, the tips of my arms could reach both sides, but the length was at least twelve feet. Despite the drought and the parched forest, it smelled of dank and despair. It was so dark in there. The walls seemed to inch closer and higher with every moment that passed.

"I almost fainted with the pain," Natasha added. "I thought you might never find me. I'd be unconscious, and you'd walk by and leave me here, and never know where I'd gone." She took a deep breath.

I squeezed her hand. "We're here. It's okay. We aren't going anywhere without you."

"Thank you," Natasha leaned her head on my shoulder, and my heart melted a tiny bit. This was the Natasha I remembered, and she was sweet, thoughtful, and kind.

I blinked back the tears. "Of course."

"Hey," Elke waved a stick at us. "Will this do?"

Natasha nodded her appreciation.

I looked up at the mound we'd come down. There was no way Natasha was limping up that. We needed another exit. I don't know if it was blind faith, or just something to focus on, but I shone my flashlight into every corner. It was so dark, it seemed like the space had to be enclosed, but there was a gap at the end, a crack in the wall, and we could maybe squeeze through it.

"No way," Natasha said when I showed it to her. "What if there's a drop on the other side?"

"Or it gets tighter, and we get stuck there forever?" Elke added.

"Okay, what do you suggest?" I frowned at their blank faces.

"Darius will come soon and look for us," Natasha said, her voice growing surer. "There's no way he'd leave me, especially if he finds the empty car."

"You sure about that?" Elke sighed. "No one's going to find us miles away from where we were headed."

"And on foot," I added like we needed it to sound worse. I was so tired of being out here lost again in the woods, only this time trapped with Natasha and Elke. I took a deep breath.

"You okay?" Natasha asked with concern in her eyes.

I nodded. Maybe this was better, as long as we made it home. Knives out, injuries healed.

"Don't focus on what we could have, or should have done. Just focus on getting out of here." Elke said. "Panic is the death of survival."

"So reassuring, you should be a life coach." But I gave her a little grin, so she'd know no hard feelings, and looked for a friendlier exit.

My feet crunched on the hard, dry earth. The air was dank down there, despite the drought. The roots from the trees above reached so far down. We were so far down. What if we didn't make it out? How would anyone ever find us? I paused for a moment to calm my racing heart. Elke was right. Panicking wouldn't help anyone. Just breathe. Take it one moment at a time. We got in, we'd get out. We had to.

"You, okay?" Elke asked.

"Totally fine." I nodded a little manically and hoped she didn't notice my lips tremble.

17

ONWARD. THAT'S WHAT I KEPT TELLING MYSELF. DON'T look at the walls bearing down on you, don't worry about the light fading, and the night falling, and the smoke, and the wildfires. Just squeeze yourself into that crack and get out of here. It sounded so simple. It was so simple.

"We are never getting out of here." Natasha hit the ground with her stick in frustration.

"Thanks, that's so helpful," Elke answered before I could. Which was probably a good thing. "That crack is the smart way out. Possibly the only way out."

"But Darius—" Natasha started.

"Won't be able to find us," Elke finished.

"She's right. Who knows how long we'd have to wait to be rescued?" I didn't want to state the obvious. No one was coming to save us.

"Go ahead then. Get us out of here." Natasha winced in pain as she tried to stretch out her leg. "I think I need an airlift."

I looked up at the hole above us. "Maybe if one of us can get out, the other can give you a boost up. The extra lift might be all we need to pull you out from the top." I doubted it. But hope was all we had right then.

Elke nodded. "Okay, Ms. Decisive, you go through the crack and report back."

I rolled my eyes. "Fine." There was no other option. That's what I kept telling myself as I shimmied up to the crack and shone my flashlight into it. The beam showed the crack opened up, wide enough for a person to slide through, maybe. The roof dipped in the middle, which was just awesome. I looked back at Elke, gesturing for me to go on, and Natasha anxiously frowning, took a deep breath, and inched my way in.

Dirt fell into my eyes, no matter how much I tried to blink it away. I wanted to go back, but it was too tight to even turn my head around. And they were there, counting on me to get through. I needed this. Mom needed this. If I didn't get back, it would kill her no matter what her diagnosis was. I stopped still. I couldn't do this. I had to do this. *Fuck!* I carried on, slowly moving through the crack sideways, a little at a time. At least I could still breathe, but how would Natasha do this?

"You okay?" Elke yelled.

"Yes!" I yelled back. Better not thinking about them waiting for me to exit or fail.

Failure was not an option.

Mom would say, "I believe in you." Just hearing her voice in my head made my heart quiver. I couldn't leave her to face the worst alone. Not knowing what had happened to her missing daughter, her only child.

"I've got this," I whispered to the walls.

Two more steps, then four more. Five more, then wait. I lifted my head up. I *could* lift my head up. The crack had widened into something more like a tunnel. My whole body fitted easily. I could breathe. I could run. I ran, tripped, got up and flew down that tunnel, all twenty feet of it and out of the entrance. I'd never been so happy to see a tangle of trees and ivy in my entire life. I shook my head and bent over gasping a few times, before realizing I had to go back in. Natasha and Elke would be freaking out.

Going in, knowing you can get out again, was a whole different experience. What seemed to take an hour coming out, took all of five minutes going back in. I was so excited we had a way out that I almost wedged myself into the tightest part, but sucked myself in, slipped my shoulders sideways, and carefully edged my way back to the pit.

"Yay, you did it!" Natasha stood, wobbled, and hugged me.

They'd both been waiting right by the crack entrance. As Elke said, listening for any signs of life. The stick worked for Natasha up to a point. She could hobble but not put any weight on her foot without gasping in pain and turning green.

"Look, I think you can make it that way, too. Then we can all get out and not have to figure out how to get you an airlift. It's only tight for a small part. Then it opens up and leads out." I realized I didn't know exactly where to. "Somewhere with trees, so not underground!" I grinned but Natasha didn't look too reassured. "We'll help you. I know you can do it."

"Let's go then," said Elke. "You first, Lily. Then Natasha, and I'll be right behind, so you can grab on to me, too."

I went back in. Natasha hopped behind me, using the stick to support her. There was no way this was going to work.

"Um, how about I hold the stick, and you squeeze in sideways with your hand on my shoulder and use me as your support?" I suggested.

Natasha looked at me like I was out of my mind. A little frown line formed between her eyes.

"It's okay, I won't let you go," I promised.

She nodded and squeezed in sideways next to me. The extra weight leaning on my shoulder almost knocked me over, but her stick in my right hand helped me balance.

"Okay, so I'm going to go really slowly. I promise you it gets better," I told her.

Natasha shuffled along one half hop at a time. Elke came behind us. All I could hear were feet shuffling in dried earth and heavy breathing. It felt like all the air was gone. My lungs panicked with each shallow breath, but that was just the tightest part. As soon as the tunnel opened, I took a deep breath. Thank God.

I took two slow steps forward with Natasha. "It's honestly not far now," I reassured her. She was holding up, jaw tensed, eyes focused on my shoulder. Her grip was strong, but I wasn't about to complain.

One last step hobble and, "Ta-da!" We came tumbling out into the woods.

"Thank God!" Natasha sat on a stump and stretched her leg out. "I thought I'd never get out of there." She turned away, clenching her fists for a moment, holding in the pain.

"I know it hurts, but your ankle probably isn't broken, or you'd never have been able to hobble like that. Can I just look and see how far the bruising goes?" I knelt down before her.

"Why? You can't do anything." Natasha shrugged. "Go on then." She raised her dress to just above her knee.

She was right, no visible bruise, and I really didn't want to take her boot off, because what if it wouldn't go back on? "Maybe it's just twisted," I said. "My mom did that once. She didn't realize there was an extra step."

"Like I didn't realize there was a six-foot hole in the ground?" Natasha rubbed her leg. "My whole leg aches."

"Probably best that you kept the boot on, but you need to see a doctor," Elke said.

"Tell me something I don't know," Natasha replied.

"Hey, I have these," said Elke, passing Natasha a couple of painkillers. "It might help with the swelling. I keep them for stress headaches."

Stress headaches were the last thing I thought Elke would get.

"Thanks," said Natasha, swallowing the tablets down dry. "I didn't think we'd make it out of there. Thank you, Lily. That was super brave." Natasha smiled, a proper warm smile that ended in a wince, but I'd take it.

"It was," Elke agreed. "Now we just need to hobble back to the car. And hope Darius is waiting there for us with a can of gas! Come on." She ducked her head as a branch almost hit her. "No rest for the wicked!"

We were deep in the woods. Different woods, with taller trees and occasional bright rust-red leaves, as if they'd been sunburned. Feet slipping on dry leaves, hands held together, we supported Natasha as she hobbled along. Slow progress was an understatement. There was nothing to follow except a vague trail, which looked more like a deer path, or maybe a route created from something bigger.

A rust-tinted moon appeared from the clouds, before rapidly being swallowed again.

"I never get used to seeing orange moons and skies. I know it happens every fire season, but it always stuns me," Natasha said, looking up at the moon.

I nodded in agreement. "Remember that time when the sky stayed orange for three days?"

"Yes," said Natasha. "That was surreal."

"That looks like a blood moon," said Elke. Trying to freak us out more than we were already. She rubbed her hands together. "I'll scout out the area and report back!" She didn't even wait for our replies before running off ahead.

Natasha raised her brows at me, and I nodded. "She'll be back."

"Yep," said Natasha. "She always is." She took a sharp breath, and I slowed our pace.

It wasn't like any of us had a clue where we were going, but Elke had more sense of direction than we had. I zipped up my hoodie tight. It was chilly and dark in the woods. Our footsteps were slow and loud, crunching leaves, breaking twigs.

A rustle came from nearby, then stopped abruptly, like something large trying to be quiet. A hunter stalking its prey. Natasha and I froze, listening.

I fumbled in my pocket and pulled out my phone. Its beam landed on two glowing eyes. They blinked and dashed up the tree. The branches swayed as they were forced aside. I shined the flashlight on the animal's bandit-masked face. Raccoon, it was just a raccoon.

I clutched my thumping chest. Jeez, all that fear for a little raccoon.

Elke burst back through the trees. "I think I know where we are. Would you rather be close to the car, or close to the road?"

It turned out we weren't close to either, but Elke had found a tree marking she was pretty sure she'd made earlier, which meant we'd gone in a semicircle. And that we had a shot at finding the Prius.

18

"IT'S OKAY, YOU KNOW," ELKE ASSURED US. "YOU JUST got to embrace the woods, don't be afraid of them. I'll guide us out. Honestly." She looked up at the sky. "The clouds don't help, but our eyes will adjust. I've been through worse."

"Like when?" Natasha asked, hopping her way over the gnarled branches. "Ouch! That hurt." She picked a bramble prickle from her arm.

"Shhh, just listen for a moment. Please," Elke added when Natasha opened her mouth to ask something else.

An owl called out and another answered. It would actually have been kind of beautiful, if we weren't stranded in the woods, with shadows and rustlings creeping around us. I shrunk into my hoodie. Thank God the storm had passed.

"Do you think it's far?" I asked, sounding like a kid on a road trip. "Sorry, I know you don't know. It's just so…"

"Creepy," Natasha finished. "Let's find shelter for the night and deal with everything in the morning. Even sleeping in the car sounds good right now."

"Yes," said Elke. "Right now, we just need to get somewhere safe."

That did not sound like a good idea to me, stuck out there in the dark. I'd feel much better if we at least found the freeway. But it wasn't like we could drive out of there. We were trapped in the woods until morning unless Darius came back. But we'd been gone so long, he would have come looking for us already, or figured we'd made it out some other way. My heart sank at the realization.

"Let's stop for a moment and check we're still going the right way. I haven't seen a tree marking in a while," said Elke. She wandered off, leaving me and Natasha standing awkwardly next to each other.

We waited, shivering, while Elke searched the nearest tree trunks for switches she might have made. My eyes adjusted to the dark. Things that were shadows before were shrubs and trees now. Logs that had fallen were clearly logs, not long arms reaching to grab me from the ground. But it still felt like we were being watched.

The hairs at the back of my neck refused to lie down, no matter what calm reasoning I pretended to have. The pine trees were so tall that I felt like I was shrinking as I stared up at the pointed tips. A bird called out, *tink, tink, tink,* and another croaked as they flew by our heads.

There was a loud crack, then a crash as a tree branch fell right in front of me. I jumped back keeping chunks of wood from hitting me.

"Holy fuck!" was all I could gasp.

"Wow!" Natasha stared at the branch. "That was so freaky!"

"Jesus!" Elke came running back "What the hell was that?"

"If I'd been an inch closer…" I couldn't finish the sentence. Elke was right. We needed to get somewhere safe. I'd shut out reality. The question wasn't if we'd get home on time or get home late; it was if we were going to get home at all. "This place is dangerous!"

"It can be," said Elke. "But it can also be kind of magical. I mean, you're okay, right? It's not like the tree attacked you."

"I could have died!" What did she not get about that?

Elke shrugged. "But you're okay. Let's keep moving." She darted ahead again, looking for confirmation that we were going the right way.

"This is not magical." I huffed, while trying to help Natasha clamber over rugged ground, downed logs, and brambles in the dark. It was a slow, stumbling progress. I shook a bug from my hair that had dropped down on me from a vine when I dared to stand still for a moment. There was a constant crunch of dry leaves, the slip of our feet, and the scurry of tiny creatures all around. A sudden owl screech made me shiver.

"Do you remember that night at camp?" Natasha asked.

"You won't let me forget it," I replied.

"No, I don't mean the fallout. You shouldn't forget that." She sniffed. "I mean the excitement of sneaking off into the woods at night, like nothing else existed, just us, and the trees and the night." She stopped to catch her breath.

I nodded. I couldn't believe she remembered it so differently. The memories came flooding back. On the bus ride over, Natasha sat with Elke at the back, laughing with the in crowd, while I sat alone at the front. Natasha messing about and kissing Elke's nose, and Elke laughing with her long blond hair loose and that look in her eye, like she knew I was watching.

Firefalls campsite in Yosemite, two to a tent, except for me. I got the smallest tent, farthest away from the bathrooms and the bear lockers. How cold it was that Yosemite night, which meant campfire fun started early. I so did not want to remember this.

The first night was all fun and s'mores, and drama-teacher-led ghost stories. The second night was pitch-black as I crept up on the secret, not-so-secret party. Every step crunched and echoed in the night. The sky was enormous and speckled with millions of stars. The Milky Way stretched across the velvet black, spinning into infinity.

And then I found them. And things got out of hand.

I pushed the images away and gripped Natasha's arm so tightly that she squealed.

"Sorry." I quickly dropped it.

"I remember," said Elke. She'd been waiting for us to catch up with her. "I can tell you do, too. It's a trauma we all share."

I'd never thought of it like that.

"I'd never been so scared," Natasha said. "I think that's why I'm okay now. I know nothing can be as scary as that."

"You're right about that," Elke agreed.

It was strangely relieving to know they'd been just as terrified. I dropped my gaze to the ground. And held everything tightly inside.

Natasha yelped as her foot caught on a root.

"Oh, God, are you okay?" Doting on Natasha was the perfect excuse to drop the conversation.

I guided her around the root clump and went much slower, kicking away as much as I could in her path. It was impossible going with just me as support. No matter how hard Natasha tried to make out she was okay, her trembling mouth showed how desperately hard she was holding in the pain.

"It's okay." I squeezed her arm. "I've got you."

She gave a faint smile and staggered on.

"Elke," I called ahead, "a little help?"

Elke stopped and flicked a leaf from her shoulder, before gently taking Natasha's other side so she could hop like a child between us. There was a low rumble in the distance. We all froze.

"I thought we'd be far away from here by now." Natasha's voice wobbled.

"It's okay, I think it was actually a plane," Elke said, looking up at the sky.

I hoped so. We could all do without the extra stress of another round of lightning storms.

"There, see"—Elke nodded to herself—"no more storm. Let's go." She carried on the slow walk, constantly glancing for clues that we were going the right way. It was so dark. The trees gathered closer around us. The path withered into a narrow trail, barely big enough for one person to follow. Three side by side was pushing it. Natasha and I were going as quickly as we could, which meant a slow, hobbling meander.

The wind gusted in the branches above and a pine cone hit my head. "Nice," I said, stooping to pick it up. That's when I noticed that just beyond the blazing red-leafed tree in front of us was a stone wall.

19

"I'LL BE TWO SECS," I SAID, RUNNING OVER TO GET A closer look.

It wasn't just a wall; it was a building made of massive stones. Just creeping closer to it gave me the chills. It was dark gray, covered in speckled silver-green lichen and ivy, and the stones were cold to the touch and pitted. It was solid and still, with a pointed roof that sloped like a child's drawing of a house. The two windows upstairs were empty, blank eyes watching out, and the gaping hole where a door once was looked ready to swallow any intruders. It was like a tumbledown version of the Hansel and Gretel cottage in the middle of the Oregon woods. The walls were scribbled halfway up with graffiti. Everything screamed "don't go in." But it was solid, and our best hope of temporary shelter.

"You need to see this!" I called out to Natasha and Elke.

As they made their way slowly through the trees, I could hear branches snap, the thump of the stick, Natasha's hopping steps, and Elke's clomping ones. If that was how noisy we'd been, it was amazing we'd seen any wildlife at all.

"What do you think?" I asked, looking up at the windows. Why did I feel compelled to stare at them? The place had obviously been abandoned long ago. "What do you think it was?"

"A witch's castle," said Elke.

"So reassuring," said Natasha. "Probably a ranger station or something like that." She hopped over closer.

It felt like there was an invisible force field between us and the house. But there was no way I was staying out there in the woods all night. We were going in.

I shivered. It must have been a good ten degrees cooler inside. There was no second floor anymore; it must have crumbled in a long time ago. The house had one large room with a tiny alcove at the back to the left. Big enough to be a pantry or a bathroom. It smelled of damp, dirt, urine, and hopelessness. There were a couple of milk crates scattered around, a few beer bottles, and a dirty sleeping bag in the corner, as if someone had stayed here overnight on a dare a long time ago. A black smudge against the wall could have once been a fireplace.

I glanced up, sure that I saw something move from the corner of my eye, something hiding in the depths of the peaked ceiling, watching, and crawling up there. A weight pushed down on my chest. I swallowed and looked down at my feet. A purple matchbox and a crumpled Doritos bag were lying there.

"I guess kids use it as a hangout," I suggested.

"Yep," said Elke swooping down the retrieve the matchbox.

"It's so creepy," said Natasha, looking up at the exact place in the ceiling where I'd seen something move. "I think there's a bat up there."

She pointed and I beamed my dwindling flashlight at it. A small bat flapped its perfect black wings and moved out of the light.

"Ah, let it be," said Elke. "This is its home we've intruding in."

It was a weird relief to know I hadn't been imagining something up there; it explained the feeling of being watched, or at least listened to.

My chest still felt super tight, perhaps from the smoke, perhaps from the effort of constantly trying to find the stupid car. "Do you both feel okay? I mean apart from your foot obviously." I grimaced at Natasha.

"I'm just really tired. What's the plan? We're not staying in this shithole, right? My foot is killing me." Natasha sat on a milk crate and rested her head in her hands.

"Perhaps just for a little while to rest it?" Elke suggested.

I nodded. I could tell Elke was eager to move on, but Natasha looked exhausted. Her eyes were shadows, and her lips a grim line. I wanted to hug her but gave her a small it-will-be-all-right smile instead. "Maybe we should sleep here for a couple of hours? It will be easier to find our way in the morning light." Better than stumbling out there in the dark.

"Yes, we're all tired," Elke agreed. "Why don't we rest here for a little while, then move on again? I mean, people obviously come here, so it can't be that deep in the forest. There must be a road or a hiking trail close by."

Elke pulled the other milk crate over and pushed it in front of Natasha. "For your foot, to elevate it. That's what you're supposed to do."

"You a doctor now?" But Natasha placed her foot on it. "I just…"

I don't know how much more of this I can take. I can't walk much farther." Natasha gave a deep sigh.

"Elke's right." I knelt next to Natasha. "You'll feel much better after resting your foot for a while." Like that would fix a sprain or fracture.

Just as I finished speaking, a roll of thunder echoed outside.

It's always worse facing things the second time. The first time you act on instinct, flight or freeze, and the relief of making it out comes afterward. But with us still being stuck there, in the tinder-dry forest, with another storm coming, the dread was real.

The first flash of lightning lit up the house.

"Wow! Lucky, we found this place!" Elke's hands flew to her heart. "I can't believe it's all starting up again."

Natasha nodded and glanced worriedly out the window. "I honestly thought we'd be out of here by now."

Thunder grumbled closer, but the building muffled it. And the lightning flashes were so much less scary when we were protected by a stone roof. We sat on cardboard, huddled next to Natasha, who was still sat on her milk crate, resting her injured foot on another.

"At least the smoke's not getting worse," said Elke. "I bet the freeway's open now." She kicked Natasha's crate gently. "That time you had those huge California fires, the smoke traveled to DC. I thought you were trying to send me a message by smoke signal."

Natasha sniffed and brushed her nose. "I did send you a message, loads of them, but you didn't even text back."

"I did. It was just a lot at first, with my dad's accident," Elke paused. "And dying." She shot a glance at me. "Then trying to figure

142

out a new place. And then I lost my phone and changed my number, but you know all that, and I'm here now. So that's all that matters, right?"

"We were so close, best friends. After you left…" Natasha's voice trailed off.

The heavy silence screamed, *This is all your fault, Lily.* I looked down at my feet and wished the cracks in the floor would widen and suck me in.

"Middle school was a bitch for everyone," Elke finally said.

Natasha smiled. "Yes, it probably is."

"I'm sorry if I hurt you. I know we were BFF close. But I was really hurting, too much to share." Elke took a deep breath. "Talking about it made it worse. It had to be just me and Mom, on our misery island. I hope you can accept that."

Natasha nodded; tears ran down her cheeks. "Of course, I do now, and I'm sorry twelve-year-old me couldn't."

They hugged, their hair falling on each other's shoulders.

I went to the door and poked my head out into the world. A roll of thunder chased itself around the clouds above. Sheet lightning lit up the sky like a firework display.

"So, what are we going to do?" I stood against the cold, bumpy wall, arms folded.

Elke sat up and pulled the joint from her pocket and rattled the matchbox. "This will help you chill." She lit it and took a deep drag, held it in, then smoothly exhaled. She passed it to Natasha, who did the same, closing her eyes as she inhaled.

She handed it on to me. I shook my head. "No thanks."

"It is pretty weak and stale." Elke stubbed it out. "I know…" Her eyes lit up. "Truth or dare."

"Ugh." Natasha rolled her eyes. "That's so boring. How about never have I ever?"

"That's even worse." I stared out the doorway. "How about three truths and a lie."

"Two truths and a lie," Natasha corrected me.

"Okay, that one," said Elke. "But let's get comfy."

I pulled over some of the less-stained cardboard for me and Elke to sit on, and Natasha shifted the milk crates around so she could lean against the wall. Elke took off her jacket and loaned it to Natasha to use for padding against the stone wall.

Another rumble came from outside, and at first, I thought it was a motorcycle, but it sounded so loud, and faded so fast, it must have been thunder.

"This will take our minds off everything," said Elke. "I'll start. Ready?"

Natasha and I nodded.

"Then I will begin."

20

ELKE CLEARED HER THROAT AND LOOKED DOWN AT THE
dirt floor. "So, number one, I was shocked to get expelled, but
relieved to go back to DC, reconnect with memories of my dad, and
not have to pretend to be happy anymore." She looked up at Natasha.

Natasha frowned and stared back.

I coughed, dry and raspy.

"You sound like you don't believe me," Elke narrowed her eyes.

"Or maybe it's your guilty conscience, jumping to conclusions." I
said, feeling like I was tiptoeing through a minefield, unsure if we had
fully disposed of all the bombs yet, with no idea when I was about
to set one off.

"Two, dropping is something I enjoy."

Natasha snorted at that. "You're supposed to be making it hard,
not easy!"

Elke gave a little smile. "Three, I wish the three of us could have
been friends in middle school, and I'm sorry I didn't invite Lily to
the bonfire party at Adventure Camp." She looked at me as if she was
testing the waters, looking for a reaction.

I didn't know what to think. She sounded genuine. But if she wishes we'd been friends, why go through with the prank? No, that didn't make any sense. That had to be the lie. A mean lie.

"Okay, who's guessing first?" Elke sat cross-legged, smug in her ability to hide her lie.

"Three," I said. "Three is a lie."

"One," said Natasha. "Dropping is in your DNA. When we first met, that was your whole persona, a nature-loving, eco geek. Sure, you loved fashion and music and all that, but at your core, you were this explorer."

Elke grinned. "I cannot possibly say who is right until you're both absolutely sure of your answers."

There was something behind Elke's eyes, a sadness. I watched as she flicked her bootlaces. Perhaps she was never as sure of herself as I thought, perhaps she was as insecure as the rest of us, just better at hiding it. She tossed back her violet hair and smiled at me, a sweet I-see-you smile.

"Oh God, I don't know now." If she'd invited me to that party, I wouldn't have felt so isolated, gone into a pious rage, and gotten Elke expelled. Or would I?

"I can see you're wavering," said Elke, with a tease in her voice.

"Okay, I'm switching to agree with Natasha." Who'd have thought it? "Because if I hadn't snitched, you'd never have got expelled, so maybe there's some truth to number three. But you've been going on and on about dropping and how you know your way around this whole time, so number one, that's the lie." I crossed my arms completely confident in my change of heart.

"Okay, drumroll!" Elke pattered on the cardboard. "And the winner is...neither of you! It was number two." She paused and actually looked worried. "I really do wish we'd been friends."

"What?" Natasha gasped. "But you love the dropping. You're always going on about all the times you went 'dropping' in the Netherlands."

Elke's voice dropped to a confessional whisper. "I only went once. It was the worst night of my life." She looked at Natasha. "Even worse than the campfire night. I wanted to be good at it, to impress my dad. It was his idea. My mom thought it was too dangerous, but I thought if I leaned more into that side, the Dutch side, he'd come back to us." Her eyes flooded with tears. "And then he would help me connect with our Moroccan family, too." She sniffed.

"I pretended to my dad that it was amazing, the best night of my life, instead of the most terrifying shit I'd ever been through, and he believed it, so I had to keep it going and make my mom believe it too, and it became part of who I was. The daredevil, adventure-seeking girl, independent, wild and free." She drew a circle on the floor. "I trapped myself into this pseudo identity because without it, who am I? I'm sorry I wanted to tell you but..." She wiped a tear from her cheek.

Natasha squeezed Elke's hand. "I wish you'd told me."

"Hah. There's no way I could tell you. Look at you. You have the perfect life: parents that adore you, a sister you idolize, and a clear path to your Stanford future. I'm Elke, the mixed-race kid, with one foot in the United States and one in the Netherlands, an outsider everywhere. Where do you come from? I don't even know. My dad knew that feeling. Moroccan Dutch isn't exactly a well-known identity outside the Netherlands, so it's easier to invent a persona. A mask." She tilted her head. "Surprise!"

"But you marked the trees, you looked at the stars," I pointed out.

"Common sense. I wish I knew more. The only thing I really learned that night is that Dutch kids are as mean as any other kids, and if you are left alone with no flashlight or cell phone, you'd better stop crying fast. And yes, your eyes really do adjust to the night."

A roll of thunder rattled overhead. It was so dark I could hardly make out their faces.

"I still can't believe that. But I understand." Natasha added quickly, "I hope I didn't make it worse for you, but I would have been your best friend no matter what. Your fake dropping skills aren't what made me love you. You don't need to hide yourself, okay?"

Elke nodded and held her lips tight.

"Also"—Natasha twisted in her seat—"I want to go next."

"Sure," said Elke with a yawn. "But don't take too long. We should try to get a few hours' sleep before dawn."

"So like you to take all the limelight and insist the rest of us rush!" But Natasha was grinning, and whatever tension had been between them before had gone. She closed her eyes, flashing them open when a draft of wind rushed through the windows, and began.

"Number one, I can't wait to go to Stanford." She peered up at us. "Number two, I think I'm in love with Darius, and I'm scared he doesn't feel the same, and that's why I broke up with him." She giggled awkwardly, like she couldn't believe she was even saying it. "And number three, I will never forgive you, Lily, for taking Elke away from me." No giggles after that.

"Jesus." I couldn't help but mutter it under my breath. Obviously, number three was true.

"I don't know, we've all come a long way." Elke raised her eyebrows at me.

"A long and winding road." Natasha laughed, then grimaced as her leg twitched. "I don't know why that's even funny."

"Sometimes crying and laughing are the same thing. My mom says that." Elke clasped her hands together. "Okay, let's crack this. You never stop going on about Stanford, even in middle school, because your super-cool, elusive sister went there, and you are desperate to follow Sophia's path."

Natasha frowned at that, but I knew Elke was right. She'd even told me Berkeley was plan B before we picked Elke up. Unless she was bullshitting everyone.

"You don't even know Darius that well, and he's been up here all summer, so it's highly doubtful you've fallen in love with him, plus you laughed," Elke pointed out.

"I agree," I said, "but why make it so easy for us? I know one and three are true, so it has to be number two!"

"Hey, hey, hey," Elke widened her eyes at me. "Slow it down. Are you sure she wasn't just trying to trick us? Maybe she *has* forgiven you." She turned to Natasha who was wriggling her sore foot. "Nope, probably not. I'll go with Lily, number two!"

Natasha took a deep sigh. "I don't even know why I'm sharing this. But you're both wrong."

"But the prank was your idea. Why did you do that if you didn't care anymore?" Elke asked.

"I'm sorry, but number three is true." Natasha rocked a little on the crate. "I tried, but I couldn't let it go. I know, it was a long time ago to you"—she turned to face me—"and I know we were once close, closer than I admitted earlier, and I'm sorry for that." She lowered her eyes. "But Elke showed me how magical a best friend could be, and in one night, you ruined everything." Her words came out in a whoosh.

"Do you even hear how that sounds? Screw this." I zipped up my hoodie and stood to go. "We used to be close, but you dropped me the minute someone better came along. How do you think that made me feel?" I was yelling at her now.

"You know," Elke said calmly, as if she was speaking to two little kids, "it's okay to have more than one friend. The problem with both of you is you love your friends with such a fierce ferocity that it can only burn out or burn you up. You both need to grow out of that."

We were silent for a moment. I glanced at Natasha. She avoided my eyes and stared up at the ceiling. "Anyway, I didn't say it was number three," she muttered.

"Wait, what?" Elke's eyes widened. "You love Darius is a lie? But I saw how you looked at him."

"No, no," I interrupted. "It's number one. You don't want to go to Stanford." These were huge bombshells being dropped. I had no idea, but I wondered how much of our true selves we'd all been hiding.

"You're right. Lily. I really thought I did want to go to Stanford, and then, I guess like you, Elke, that became part of my identity, and it was hard to let go. Everyone always asks, what do you want to do, go to Stanford like your sister, Sophia? Not my mom and dad. They're supportive of whatever I want to do. But I didn't want to let them down either. They don't know I haven't even applied." She shut her mouth fast and took a deep swallow. "And Sophia was so excited to show me around that I pretended to be excited about it, too. It's easier to go along with what everyone expects you to want than to decide what you really want, you know?"

I knew that feeling. I was so ready to move forward, blaze a new path at Oak Canyon College, and leave the past behind. But with Mom's "not what we hoped for news," my dream was impossible. My heart sank. "But sometimes dreams only get broken."

"I get you, Lily. But you have to fight for them, right?" Natasha said it like she believed it was all possible.

I frowned. I'd had too much experience with what dreaming the impossible brings: disappointment and heartache.

"And Natasha, that goes doubly for you. if you love Darius, why give up at the start?"

Natasha sighed. "It's stupid to begin your college years attached to a boy." The way she said *boy*, like he was so much more than that, clutched at my heart. "If I even go to any college. It's just not going to work. So why pretend? It's better to kill it and not break his heart."

"That's why you stayed behind while I got lost chasing Lily," said Elke. "Because you were arguing, and that's why you were being such a cow to him. But the heart wants what the heart wants, and he doesn't want to end things!" Elke grinned.

"Yes, and now I just want to say sorry and make up, if we ever get out of this shithole." Natasha let out a huge sigh. "I feel like I'm in a therapy session." She turned to me. "Honestly, I already do forgive you a little."

"Baby steps," I said as if I forgave her, too.

The wind whooshed around outside, shaking the treetops. A clap of thunder made us all jump. The storm was getting worse, but at least we were out of it, baring our souls in here.

I took a deep breath, unsure of what I was even going to say. "Okay, my turn. One, there's no way I'm ever going to college because Mom got half a message through, and it sounds like her cancer is bad." I let out a big sigh. It was a relief to say that out loud.

"But she wants you to go, right?" asked Elke.

"Yes, but how can I?" I stared at the lichen-covered wall.

"Ohh-kay," Elke said, in a way that meant she didn't think it was okay at all.

"Two," I said, sliding right on through. "I yelled, 'Fire!' because there was one, and people could have gotten hurt." This was hard. "I was sick of everyone talking about how amazing and what fun you were, and you didn't even invite me to the stupid midnight party." Wow, that was out. "I didn't mean to panic everyone." I looked directly at Elke. "I didn't mean for you to be expelled." It was a perfect storm of pent-up emotions, and once I'd set everything in motion, it was unstoppable. "I just wanted to punish Natasha. I'm truly sorry. I get it if you can't forgive me, but that doesn't change how sorry I am." I stared at the floor, willing my tears to not flood out. "And three, I wish to God I'd never accepted the stupid ride."

"Oh no, no. no, you don't get to make a huge statement about number two, and not let us address that first!" Elke stood up and hugged me so tightly that tears leaked out of my eyes. She whispered in my ear, "I know girl crushes are the worst." Then she let me go and smiled. "Middle school is the pits. Who knows why we did half the things we did? That midnight party, and the fire, were stupid ideas, but I was too naive to know that." She glanced at Natasha.

"Okay, yes, I didn't invite you. That was on me. I didn't want you there. Sorry." Natasha didn't sound remotely sorry. "I was just a fierce friend. Tween girls are the worst." She shrugged. "Still, you did get Elke expelled, and you did start the panic."

"I didn't mean to."

"You didn't think shouting, 'FIRE! FIRE!' would start something?" A little line ran along Natasha's forehead. "If you hadn't told on us for the stupid bonfire, they wouldn't have searched our tent and found the vodka, and Elke would never have moved back to DC."

"You're still blaming me, even though it was your bonfire and your booze." I slumped against the wall. "I'm so done with this."

"Me too. Seriously, stop defending me." Elke tilted her head at Natasha. "I love you, Natasha, but please let it go. And Lily, forgive us for our misguided prank, and I forgive you"—she grinned—"for luring me into the forest." She said it like I was some kind of temptress.

Natasha sighed. "Okay, all forgiven." What choice did she have?

"Forgiven," I agreed. There was nothing to lose. If we got out of here in one piece, we'd never see each other again anyway.

"So, what one is it?" Natasha asked.

"Nope, we've got to guess," said Elke. She studied my face carefully. "I say number three is a lie because actually you were dying to see me again," and she grinned at me.

"Seriously?" Natasha sniffed. "I bet she's right."

"She is," I admitted. "But not for that reason. Just, it feels good to talk it out and forgive each other. And that never would have happened if we hadn't got stuck out here."

"Let's hug it out," said Elke, swooping the three of us together.

She squeezed us so hard that we had no choice but to relax into it. And for the first time it really felt like a new beginning. Natasha even gave me a small smile, and I couldn't help but smile back. We'd never be best friends again, but a nod in the school hallways would be good enough for me.

"It's midnight already," Elke said with a big yawn. "Let's get some sleep, just a couple of hours."

Too tired to reply, we nodded and gathered our belongings together—a water bottle, a backpack, and Elke's jacket—and made a little nest on the floor. Natasha moved from the crate to the floor so she could huddle with us, making a pillow for her injured foot with Elke's backpack. I yawned and Natasha and Elke caught it, as we leaned on each other and closed our eyes.

I remember thinking there was no way I'd actually fall asleep like that with thunder still rumbling around outside and wind gusting through the doorway, but somehow we all did.

MIDNIGHT

21

A CRASH OF THUNDER SENT ME STUMBLING TO MY KNEES.
For a second, I couldn't even remember where I was. Gray stone walls loomed above me, and a crack of lightning lit up the empty windows. Oh yes, the witch's castle. I shivered. It was still dark outside, and freezing inside.

Elke squeezed my arm to say hi, as Natasha mumbled in her sleep.

There was another sound. Footsteps and an angry bark.

A German shepherd came racing through the dark toward us, ears pointed, teeth bared.

"He won't bite, as long as you don't move!" a man's voice yelled.

We froze on the spot as he stepped in. He was a disheveled old man who wore a furry hat over his white tufts of hair and a green padded jacket. He had a dead rabbit draped over one hand and a rifle in the other.

I could not take my eyes off that gun.

"Hunter, Hunter, stay." The dog went over and stood near the entrance, blocking us in. Saliva dripped from its mouth, and its eyes held our motionless reflections in its fierce gaze.

Natasha reached for Elke's hand, and Elke gripped mine.

"Don't worry, nothing's going to happen to you. Not while I'm here." The old man clicked his pale, mottled fingers and pointed at the corner near the alcove. Hunter went straight to it and sat down. "Good boy." He turned slowly to look at us. "To what do I owe the pleasure of your company?"

His ripped, thick jeans were stained with grass and something darker, mud or blood.

A clap of thunder clashed above us.

"It's a bad night to be roaming the woods alone," he said, putting the rifle down against the wall by the dog. "Lucky you found this place."

None of us spoke.

"Don't be afraid." He placed the rabbit on a hook and took off his overcoat, folding it carefully before placing it on the floor. He gestured for us to sit on it.

I barely held in a shudder.

"We were just going," said Elke, finally breaking our silence.

"That's a terrible idea. I can't possibly let you do that." He smiled, showing his yellowed teeth. For a minute I thought he was joking, but then I glanced at the dog. It raised its ears, tracking our every move.

Elke smiled, as if she wasn't worried. "We didn't know this was your place, and we're sorry for that, but we were just leaving, *are* leaving." And she took a step to the door.

In a flash the dog was there. It didn't bark or even growl; it just stood there blocking our exit, watching, and waiting for his owner's command.

The man narrowed his eyes, as if he wasn't quite sure what Elke had just said. He tilted his head. "Do you not hear the storm out there?"

Thunder rumbled above us, and wind whooshed around the top of the stone walls, rattling the ivy that clung to the roof.

"We thought we'd make a run for it," Natasha added.

"Oh, no, sit for a while and wait for the storm to pass. You don't want to be trapped out there with lighting striking trees all over the place. Never know what might happen, and I'd never forgive myself if something did."

True, I'd come close to that already without the storm's help. But still. "We'll just take our chances, thank you," I added, with that curt British politeness that always came out whenever I was stressed. My Scottish gran would have been proud.

I gave a fake smile to Natasha, motioned to the door with my eyes, and the three of us made our way over to it.

"That's a really bad idea," the old guy said.

The dog growled and licked its lips.

"Fuck's sake." Elke glared at the old man. "Dude, you cannot be serious. This is entrapment."

"Come on, you'll catch your death out there." He spoke softly, as if he was being perfectly reasonable. Perhaps he thought he was. "I'm just trying to help you help yourselves."

A flash of lightning blinded us for an instant with its white-hot brightness. The dog jumped back, and for a second I thought it was in attack mode, but it regained its composure and stood at the entrance again, although every hair on its body was raised.

"Please," he added, "do what you like, but as someone who knows these parts better than my own whiskers, wait until the lightning passes, then go."

He gave me a wink, like that would make me feel any less creeped out.

I looked at the dog. "Hey, Hunter," I said, holding out my hand.

It didn't budge. If a dog could give the side-eye, that's what it was doing, but at least it hadn't bitten me. Yet.

"Don't waste your time on him. He's a one-man dog. Why don't you sit down, make yourselves at home? I can probably rustle up a drink or something while you wait. Three young girls out in the woods all night, you must be starving." The old guy went back to the alcove, safe in the knowledge we weren't leaving with his dog guarding the door.

I looked at Elke, and she shrugged. Natasha shook her head. The gun was right there. I took a step toward it. Hunter growled. I stepped back. I didn't know what I'd do with it, anyway, shoot myself probably. I rolled my eyes and gave up. He was just an old guy, trying to stop us from going out in the storm and being struck by lightning. Not a murderer, just homeless and lonely. Probably.

Elke and I sat on the cardboard, and Natasha hobbled her way back to the milk crates.

"My name's Neil, by the way," he called back to us. "Old Neil, if you're a friend, and Crazy Neil, if you're not." He came back to us with three tin mugs of water and pulled a silly face. "Keeps the tourists away from the place." He grinned. "Now, you are obviously not tourists, so what are you doing out here on a night like this?"

I accepted the water and passed another to Elke, and Natasha took hers. None of us drank.

"We got lost," Elke said, "in the storm and she hurt her foot."

We all stopped to look at Natasha's foot. You couldn't really tell anything was wrong, unless you noticed her wince every time she moved it.

"Bad, is it?" he asked.

"I almost blacked out when it happened," Natasha admitted.

"I've got something for you." He wondered back to the alcove. I regretted not bothering to look back there when we'd come in.

A few moments later, he wandered back again and handed Natasha two metal hiking sticks and a pack of ibuprofen. "You'd be amazed what I find in these woods. Two of those will help reduce the inflammation, and the sticks will help you walk without putting weight on it."

A chill passed through me. Who leaves their hiking sticks behind?

"People go missing out here all the time," he said. "As soon as the storm stops, you need to get out of here, get that leg seen to."

As if we hadn't thought of that.

"Yes, I will," said Natasha, and gave a tight smile.

"You got a car?" He leaned forward.

We all leaned back.

"Yes," said Natasha.

"No," Elke and I said, which was technically true, but confusing.

"I see," Neil nodded. "You're still a bit unsure about me. I don't blame you. Don't trust strangers, and all that, but you're here in my place, and did I chase you out? *No*, I invited you *in*, gave you *drinks*.

161

So, why would I be anything else but kind?" He looked from me to Natasha, and then to Elke. "How did you three meet then? What are you doing out here in the wild, wild woods?"

He noticed me looking at the gun. "Oh, that's just for hunting. You saw the rabbit. A man's got to eat, and a dog, too." He grinned at Hunter. "Here, boy." Finally, Hunter left his guard post to sit beside his owner.

I glanced at Elke, who nodded toward the door. Natasha saw and held her hand tight, not yet. I took a sip of water and spat it out. It burned my throat.

"Nothing like a touch of moonshine to see you through the night." Neil laughed.

Oh, so funny. "It's an acquired taste, I guess." I placed the mug down on the dirt floor. "We met at school, middle school," I said, "to answer your question."

The wind grew wilder, blowing around the walls like some huge animal stalking outside.

"We're carpooling home," said Natasha. "I expect out parents will be worried about us by now," she added.

"Sending search parties," Elke said hopefully.

"Not with this storm and the fire danger. All hands on deck making sure no fires break out and the power grid isn't affected. And even in less fraught times, it takes a long time to convince the sheriff anyone's truly missing out here, and not just wanting not to be found, or on their way home again already. And they're stretched so thin that it takes forever for search parties to get started, and even longer for anyone to get found alive. There's plenty of accidental deaths out here. Too many don't make it. One small mistake can make the difference between life and death." Neil crossed his arms and sighed.

I shivered. This night was going from bad to worse.

"That's why I'm so glad you found me." He smiled and cracked his knuckles. "You're safe now. Isn't that right, Hunter?"

He scratched Hunter's ears. Hunter wagged his tail like he was in heaven, but he never took his eyes off us. His ears flicked with every move we made, no matter how small.

"And if the crevasses and cliff edges don't get you, the hunters will," he added. Like he'd said nothing mind-blowing at all.

I swear I heard the faint crack of branches breaking between every thunderclap. I didn't know what was more dangerous, being out there in the woods, or in there with Neil, and his gun, and his dog.

"So," said Elke, "how long have you been following us?"

22

"I'VE GOT BETTER THINGS TO DO THAN CHASE AFTER YOU three. Hunting dinner for a start." He stared at Elke. "What made you think that anyway?"

"You mentioned the cliff edges. The crevasses, like you knew where we'd been." Elke recrossed her legs as she spoke.

"You have been there, haven't you? Too deep in the woods and a little too close to the edge." He stopped, as if he'd realized his mistake.

Elke and I exchanged a glance.

"So, you saw me slip?" I asked.

He shook his head, unconvincing. "No, that's just a figure of speech. I didn't follow you. Those are just some of the things that happen to people who aren't used to these woods. If you weren't lost, you never would have found this. It's off the beaten track for a reason, and yet,"—he leaned in closer, dropping his voice to a whisper— "you'd be amazed how many people find it!"

Hunter whimpered slightly and lay down, as if he knew it was story time. We all did the same; it was pointless not to. At least until the storm stopped crashing right outside.

"There was this one time," Neil continued, "a father and daughter came by, looking for shelter. She wasn't more than seven years old, and her dad looked scared, as if he was being hunted. I showed them the cave. More of a crack in the ground really, but they rested there a while. I made them a roof of leaves and branches, took them water, and gave them fried rabbit. But the next day when I went back, they were gone. They left these hiking sticks, which is odd, but I took it as payment, a thank-you."

The cave sounded awfully like the crevasse Natasha fell into. Perhaps it wasn't a trap after all. But why didn't he just bring them here?

"What about fires tonight? Is it just Wolf Hollow that's spread?" The pit of my stomach flipped.

"That's not the fire you should worry about. The firefighters are on it already. It's the small ones in the valleys, hidden until it's too late. The campfires that get out of control and make the RVs' propane tanks explode."

I dared not look at Natasha or Elke.

Neil carried on. "One stray spark and *whoosh*, the whole forest goes up! That's when you get a whole load of fires, and the fire service is too stretched to catch them all. Add to that the ones who love to set a little fire here, a little fire there, and before you know it, the whole forest's blazing and the fire travels too fast for everyone to get out. Don't worry though, you're safe here. Fire won't burn these stones down." He grinned and ruffled Hunter's head. "Isn't that right, boy, safest place to be in the whole forest."

"How did you end up here?" Natasha asked.

"That's not something I tell people I only just met," he said. "Got to earn my trust before I reveal my deepest, darkest secrets."

Natasha nodded as if that was totally understandable but flashed me a *help* look. She wanted out of there as much as I did. Elke looked unconcerned, watching a spider work its way across the room on worried legs.

A blast of wind blew in around the top of the building, bringing with it the faint smell of smoke. There was either a new fire or Wolf Hollow was still spreading.

Neil followed my gaze. "The wind's picking up. Going to be a gnarly night tonight."

I bit my lip, sure that here was not the best option. My knee shook. Every part of my body was tensed to run. I glanced at Elke.

She shook her head and asked him, "Do you have many dark secrets to tell?"

Jesus, Elke! Natasha and I exchanged a WTF look. Did we want to know the answer?

Neil frowned. "I doubt it," he said. "Not compared to a lot of people. You'd be surprised at the people I meet out here and their reasons for not wanting to be found."

I thought of the missing person flyers we'd seen.

"And you help them disappear?" Elke leaned in closer.

"I keep them safe." Neil frowned back at her. "Like you three here now, safe from the storm."

Natasha kept repositioning her leg. Every time our eyes met, I saw the same fear that I felt. The smoke scent was getting stronger. We couldn't just sit here waiting for the worst.

I gestured to Natasha and Elke we should go. But as soon as I moved, Hunter's heckles went up, and he growled low and fierce. *Shit.* I huddled in my hoodie, as if it was protective armor that could stop a dog from biting me.

Thunder slammed against the walls. A flash of lightning, followed quickly by another. If I never saw another thunderstorm in my whole life, that would be fine by me. The walls were so thick and old, I wondered what stories were trapped in there, and if we would be one of them. I shook my head. No, we were going to get away.

"Nasty night you picked. Where was I? Oh, yes, all the missing people. I don't know what happened, but these woods... Lots of people live in there, and they don't want to be found. Don't go knocking on their doors for help, or you'll disappear fast as a lightning strike." He gestured with his hands. "*Poof!* Gone, and no one will ever find you."

"Oooo-kay, thanks for the warning," said Natasha. "Thank you for everything, but we really should be going." And she rose, all shaky on one leg, and tried to put her weight on the other. She gasped out in pain and sat again. Elke rushed to help her, and I grabbed the hiking sticks.

"Hey, they're no good for walking outside right now," he said, watching her make slow progress toward the doorway. "The last thing you need is to attract lightning."

I stood there, unsure what to do. Natasha trembled as she glared at him. Hunter barked as if he was waiting for orders. Natasha sat back down on the crate, gasping as Elke accidentally knocked her foot.

"Sorry." Elke's whole face scrunched with worry. "Are you okay?"

Natasha sighed and shut her eyes. Elke sat back down on the floor next to her and rubbed her arm. I sat with the hiking sticks by my side. So much for that escape attempt.

"Not my fault, just trying to help," Neil said, like he was enjoying humbling her, us.

This was a never-ending nightmare. We were stuck and not stuck. I couldn't decide who Neil was, or what he wanted from us. Why he kept us trapped there, or if we were even really trapped. I couldn't even decide if he was deliberately trying to freak us out or was just a sweet, bumbling old man who lived in the woods. Were we going to sit there forever waiting to find out?

I could see Natasha looking at the door, and Elke fiddling with her hands in her pockets. It made me do the same, and that's when I found the stick of jerky.

"So, you're best staying the night. If you go into the woods, you'll only get lost, fall, or be shot at by some hunter." He glanced at his gun, then tapped another pinch of tobacco out of his bag as if he hadn't said anything threatening at all.

And if he wanted to help us so much, why didn't he help when we thought we'd gotten stuck in the crevasse? Elke's eyes were as wide as mine. Did he even realize what he'd said?

He looked at Natasha. "Good for you getting this far." He patted his dog. "Plenty fall and can't walk out again. Isn't that right, Hunter?" *That far.* He knew exactly where we'd been.

I should have been scared, but the thing that sent chills up my spine was disappearing and Mom never knowing what happened to me. No way was I going to let that happen. I murmured to Elke. "We've got to get out of here."

168

She gave me a *duh* look but nodded like she was working on it. I kept looking for possible escape routes. Maybe we could just race for the doorway, but he had that gun and that ever watchful dog. Hunter's tongue lolled to the side; drool pooled off it. He snapped this jaw shut and looked at me with hungry eyes. Hungry, that was it.

I nudged Elke and subtly pulled out a corner of jerky. Her eyes widened. I mimicked "run" with my fingers. She glanced at Natasha and then at the door. Natasha gave the tiniest nod that she understood.

God, we were really doing this. In one swift move, I pulled the jerky from my pocket and threw it at Hunter, ran to Natasha, pushed the hiking sticks into her hands, and pulled her to her feet.

Elke kicked the gun under a pile of rags and rushed to support Natasha on her other side. We fled, if staggering lopsidedly with Natasha between us, can be called fleeing.

"You're going to regret it!" Neil called out after us. He didn't even get up.

Natasha spun around. "Stop being ridiculous. You think we're going to stay with you because you're threatening us with your dog, and your gun, and saying if we leave, we'll be struck by lightning? You think this place won't be swarming with police and volunteers looking for us come daybreak?" Natasha scowled. "Not that it's okay to treat anyone this way. If you were trying to help us, then help. Don't pretend you care if you don't. Come on." She turned to us. "Enough of this, we're leaving!"

Elke and I watched in amazement. This was the Natasha we loved and adored. The badass who wasn't taking shit from anyone.

The last glimpse I got of him, he was shaking his head and laughing to himself. But I also heard the *click-click* of a gun being reloaded.

23

WE RAN-HOBBLED INTO THE TREES. NATASHA LEANED against me, got her hiking stick caught on a tree root, fell, and hopped on. She'd be the first to get caught if Neil did come after us. Elke disappeared ahead into the forest.

Somehow it came back to me, while I was supporting Natasha with one hand and flicking a spider off the back of my neck with the other, that in middle school Elke had drawn forest scenes all over her language arts folder—sinewy trees, birds, mushrooms, and big-eyed deer, like a fairy tale. Natasha had said it was part of Elke's Dutch culture.

And that's when kids started calling her Viking. It didn't matter that the Dutch weren't even Vikings. It sounded edgy and cool, and Elke lived up to that image. Every day a new revelation: how many languages she knew (three), how many countries she'd lived in (five), and how many people had instant crushes on her—guys and girls—so many. I wouldn't have minded any of that, if it hadn't been that Natasha only had eyes for Elke. It all seemed so stupid and irrelevant now. But at the time it felt like Elke had stolen my entire life. And now here we were, working together to save each other. At least I hoped that's why Elke had run ahead.

I held Natasha's arm tighter, helping her keep her balance as she struggled to get over the bumpy ground on one good leg. Hiking sticks are not that helpful when you can't see where on the ground to place them.

I couldn't tell if Neil or Hunter were behind us. It was just me and Natasha together like one gangly human-and-a-half, staggering and crashing our way through the undergrowth.

"Thank you," she whispered.

I nodded. "Of course." It was true, there was no way I'd leave her behind. Whatever happened, the three of us were bonded together now. I fought my way through low-hanging branches, tripped on the bumpy ground, and tried not to imagine Neil silently stalking us the whole time.

Elke was back. "Get down," she hissed.

"Ouch," Natasha gasped as Elke pushed her against a tree trunk.

"Shush." Elke held her finger to her lips, then ducked right down, cheek next to mine, violet hair tickling my chin.

I dared not move. Our hearts pounded on top of each other. I could smell the pink icing of the dope doughnut on Elke's breath. I closed my mouth, aware that it was suddenly so close to hers. My arm twitched. She squeezed it tightly in a way that meant don't move, don't make a sound. Footsteps marched past, followed by a dog padding behind. Neil was sprightlier than he looked.

"Safest if you stay with me," he called out. "Didn't mean to scare you!"

Well, he was doing a good job now. We stayed rigidly in place. A beetle scuttled across my leg. I didn't even flinch, just bit my lip and screwed my eyes shut, and concentrated on the sound of the wind rattling the leaves. Neil's footsteps faded away.

"That was close," I whispered.

"What if he really was just trying to help?" asked Natasha.

"What, with a gun?" I asked.

"What if we die out here?" Natasha looked down at her foot.

"Don't be silly." I took another few tentative steps. I grabbed her arm to steady her. "See, I've got you." She had the grace not to laugh.

"People *do* die out here—not just runaways, but experienced hikers and hunters. They disappear and never get found, but their stuff is all there, backpacks, wallets, car keys, cars still there abandoned." Elke's voice echoed in the dark adding weight to her words.

"Are you saying it's Neil?" I asked.

"No, but someone. Or maybe a group of someones. It just seems like there are too many missing to be a coincidence."

"Stop trying to freak us out." Natasha's voice trembled at the end, possibly from the strain on her leg, possibly not. "I just hate to think I misjudged him."

"You were pretty brave back there," I said to her.

"Thanks. I'd had it with this whole night, and sometimes my anger tips me over to do things I don't normally have the nerve to." She smiled. "Could have gone badly wrong."

"Still might," Elke said, as if we needed reminding.

"Whatever, he won't tangle with you, so that's good." I pointed out. But what if Elke was right? What if the disappeared were out there listening to us? I glanced anxiously at the darkness behind the trees—the darker dark, the blackest black of hidden rustling watching things. "How do you know all this anyway?" I asked Elke.

"Google 'missing people Oregon.' It's worse than any horror story. Some go missing straight from Eugene—where you picked me up."

There was a crack in the undergrowth. We froze. There it was again. Someone was there, watching us.

"What do we do?" I mouthed.

"Wait," Elke whispered. She turned around slowly to the last spot we heard anything.

A deer jumped out and stared at us, looking something between annoyed and embarrassed, flicking its black-tipped ears. We stepped back waiting until it bounded into the trees.

"That was intense!" The cool night air crawled under my skin and sent goose bumps across my arms. "Hey"—I looked at the sky—"did you notice, no thunder?" I waited expecting to be wrong. But I was right. The storm had stopped. Finally!

"Come on, let's find the stupid car!" Elke took Natasha's other arm so she could hop freely between us and grasped the hiking sticks in her other hand. "These are useless in the dark."

"Do you think I didn't notice? Ouch, careful," Natasha said after bashing her foot against a tree stump.

Elke sniffed the air. "That smoke's getting stronger. We need to move fast."

She was right. The farther away from the witch's castle we got, the thicker the smoke, until it hung like a heavy veil over the trees. It was too close to be from the Wolf Hollow fire.

I coughed. My lungs struggled to get enough oxygen from the smoky air. "Shit, it's got to be really close."

"Listen," Elke cocked her head. There was faint hum of a motor.

"Darius?" said Natasha hopefully.

Elke shook her head and pointed to the sky, just in time to see a plane fly overhead releasing a trail of retardant. "If the plane's going that way, we should be going the other way."

"We should be going wherever the Prius is," I pointed out. "Anyway, I thought you were the forest expert."

"Touché. Kick me while I'm down."

We walked on a little in silence. The hair on my neck stood on end. It felt for sure like we were being followed, but every time I swung around, there was nothing.

Elke reached over and squeezed my shoulder, "It's okay. Neil wouldn't follow us this far."

"Or Hunter," I added. We'd have heard the dog by now. He'd be begging for more jerky or trying to snap my face off.

Elke tripped over and almost fell. "There is no flat ground here."

I stopped. The sky on the top of the ridge was a rich blood-orange as smoke billowed thick and brown. "There's got to be a new fire up that way." I pulled my brown hoodie tighter.

"Should we go back and try to warn Neil?" Natasha looked back to the trail we'd come on.

"No, we don't even know where we are. And he knows his way around," I said. Unlike us.

"Stay calm." Elke looked back at the ridge. "We're going to figure it out. We're still going the right way, well away from the fire. We'll keep that ridge to our backs and let someone know about Neil once we get out of here."

The smoke hovered over the ridge like a shroud. It was still early, or was it late? I checked my phone, just past four thirty. Still no signal.

"That smoke's getting worse," Natasha pointed out. "I think it's from a new fire."

"I think so, too." I remembered Darius's warning about not wanting to be stuck between two fires.

"It's a different kind of smoke." Elke actually looked worried.

"And it's getting thicker," said Natasha. "We need to go faster, and I can't." She was right, but we weren't about to admit it.

Wind flurries blew smoke into our eyes. A faint sound of wailing came toward us, then sped by. A fire engine.

"There's got to be a road straight ahead!" I pointed in the direction of the sound. "Fire trucks need roads."

We came out from the dense trees to a wider path. We'd been going downhill so long that we could turn back and see the ridge we'd come from, and just behind that another hill with a deep amber glow behind it, like the sun had just set, only it hadn't. And sunrise was hours away. It was eerie and surreal. I couldn't stop staring at it.

Elke yanked me away. "Look, a sign!"

WOLF HOLLOW STATE FOREST
FIRE DANGER HIGH.

Thanks for that. At least we had to be on a trail.

175

I grinned. "Civilization is just around the corner!" Yes, I was a little excited.

"Let's go!" Natasha even got a new burst of energy.

We scurried along, stopping every now and then to check we were still on the trail, fumbling our way over hillocks, tree stumps, ferns, and roots, past a burned-out truck and a flattened abandoned tent. We had to be close.

The smoky air made my eyes teary. And every time I looked back at the smoke, it had got denser. What if we couldn't find the car? What if we couldn't outrun a fire?

"There!" Elke pointed. "A light!"

Just visible through the sepia haze was a dim yellow light. As we got closer, we realized it was shining through an RV window.

24

THE LIGHT SEEPED THROUGH THE RAGGED BLINDS THAT partially covered a cracked pane. The temporary solution of resting the RV on breeze blocks had become permanent, judging by the sporadic way they stuck out and the dirt with weeds nestled in them.

The whole thing looked like one big puff of wind could blow it over, and it would be on its back like a beetle wriggling its legs. But it was here, occupied, and maybe whoever lived there could get us out of this smoke.

"They have to know the way out, right?" asked Natasha.

"Are we doing this?" Elke asked, poised ready to knock.

I nodded. "It's our best option."

"Only option," Natasha confirmed.

"Okay then." Elke drew herself up and knocked, quietly at first, then louder. It sounded tinny. The door wobbled as she knocked it, like it might fall open by itself. "Maybe no one's home."

"Why leave the light on, unless it's to make it look like someone's there?" I asked.

There was a thump. Followed by a heavy silence.

"Maybe they're just checking who we are," suggested Natasha. "Scary strangers or lost teens?"

"Yes," I agreed. "Though I don't know how they'll see anything in this smoke." I knocked again, a gentle, friendly *tap, tap, tap-tap-tap*. "Hello?" I called.

There was another small thump. We waited, eyes glued to the door.

"We can maybe get a ride or call an Uber." I sighed at the thought. "No more walking through forests." I hadn't thought about my phone in a while. At least Mom would hopefully be asleep and not worrying about me. There was nothing I could do, except make sure I got home.

"They're not going to have Ubers way out here," said Elke. "And there's nothing wrong with walking through forests."

"But maybe not with all this smoke!" I said as I slipped my phone away.

"Do you think they even know there's a fire nearby?" Natasha asked.

"How could they not have noticed?" I knocked politely on the door again.

Nothing.

Natasha pounded on the door. "Open up! We need help!"

"Go away!" It was an old woman's voice. "We don't want you here."

That shocked us all. For a moment we just stood there, gazing at the dirty metal door.

"Do you think that's what Neil was warning us about, people that don't want to be found?" I whispered.

"There's a wildfire close by!" Elke shouted at the door.

No response.

"Screw it then." Elke took Natasha's arm. "Come on, we're on our own, or all together." She frowned. "Would you rather be on your own, or all together?"

"Together," I said without hesitation.

"Agreed," said Natasha. "No one gets left behind." Her copper eyes searched mine. "All past events forgiven."

Elke nodded. "Let's draw a line right here." She drew a fake line on the ground. "We leave our past on the other side of the path. All the shitty things we've all done, even ones from earlier today. I know some are worse than others, but we're leaving them here, outside this RV because we will never be as awful as the people inside there."

"Fine," said Natasha.

"And we swear to have each other's backs, no matter what happened before," said Elke.

"Deal," I said.

Natasha echoed it. "Deal."

I gave a long sigh. It was a relief to let that all go, all the past, all the shame, all the resentment.

A branch flew in the wild wind, bouncing right off the metal walls. You could almost see the particles of smoke in the air, brushing everything sepia.

"Let's go!" Elke yelled.

We limped on. Exhausted, but somehow at peace. We'd found a trail. We'd find the road. We'd definitely be out of there before the new fire caught up with us. Wherever that fire was. I tried not to think about that too hard, but focused on moving on, one small target at a time. First find the road, second find the car, third get out of there.

We established a pattern. Elke and I would take a step and stop for Natasha to hop and swing. It was way faster than before, a persistent flounder forward, rather than a stagger and stop. The wind sent branches, leaves and bits of dirt flying and twisting up in the air.

We hurried along, stopping at each scuttle, each animal cry, trying and failing to hear anyone else. My stomach was a knot of worms. The night lay heavy on my shoulders. The acrid smoke coated the inside of my nose. I could hardly breathe. We had to make it to the road, even if we didn't find the car.

"This way," Elke pointed to a smaller path to the left. "Yay! A tree with a mark! We're on the right path, for sure."

"How the hell?" I shook my head.

"Don't question just follow," Natasha said. "Luck of the Vikings." And we all laughed and then coughed and then laughed again. Until Natasha hit her leg on a tree and had to stop to yelp.

A coyote howled back.

We staggered on, faster now we were sure we were going the right way. It's amazing what a little hope can do to spur you on. I glanced at Elke, she grinned back.

This was really happening. We could really be friends. I licked the blood from my lip.

"See, here," Elke pointed at the ground. "My beautiful Doc Martens footprints!" There was an imprint in the dry dirt.

Another siren wailed in the air. We were so close! Once found, our tracks were easy to follow. The car would be low on gas, but Elke figured if we could just get it to a road, we could flag down someone to take us to the gas station. And failing that, it was shelter.

My instincts tingled, the hairs on my arms stood to attention, and it wasn't just from the lightning. A sixth sense was warning me, the kind survivors talk about listening to. The kind that prevents them from walking into death's path. A low thrum filled the air. And I couldn't tell if it was a sound or a vibration.

An ember swirled by, like a brilliant firefly. It landed on the trail in front of us and ignited a shriveled brown fern. I froze as it scurried up the whole stem, glowing with flickering orange fingers. My skin crawled with déjà vu. The bad kind, the reliving-your-nightmare kind.

"Shit!" Elke ran over to stamp it out.

I ran to help seconds later. Seconds that meant it had spread across the ground, igniting dried grass on its way. We stamped and stamped, until every spark was dead.

"Oh my God," Natasha's voice shook. "See, how you can freeze and not mean to?"

I nodded but I didn't hear her. *The spark.* My insides trembled. I forced my mind to stay blank. *Do not, do not, do not, go back to that night.*

Natasha shook her head. "Oh my God, it was just like back then, remember?"

No. I do not. I just gave her a blank look. It was all I could manage.

She carried on, "I mean that night, when that spark caught hold of that leaf and then jumped onto the tree, and it glowed bright orange all the way up the trunk, and then it split in two, and everyone just stared, and the wind whisked those sparks, and suddenly everyone was running and screaming, and it seemed like the whole camp was on fire?" She paused, to stop herself hyperventilating.

Elke nodded. "That was some night."

They were both looking at me, waiting for my response.

"I was really scared," I said quietly. "The fire spread so fast. I thought we might die." I'd never admitted that before, not even to myself. I'd told Mom it was fine, a minor incident that got blown up out of proportion. She was already so sick I didn't want to stress her. Anyway, no one got hurt. Not physically.

"Me too. It was wild," said Elke. "I saw how it started."

"You made the fire, so you should know." Obviously.

"Yes, but I didn't spread it. You remember, don't you?" Elke's eyes bored into mine. "That night." I wasn't sure what she meant. But I was sure by her insistence there was something I was missing.

Natasha grabbed Elke's hand. "Let's get out of here. You can figure all this from the car."

"One sec," Elke pulled her hand away. "Tell me, Lily?"

I shook my head. This couldn't be happening. I remembered nothing. Not the pitch-black night, the crunch of my steps, the laughter. Not the scent of dank bark as I hid in the shadows. It wasn't me. These weren't my memories. I was no longer that girl.

Natasha looked from me to Elke. "Come on, whatever this is can wait."

That spark. I caught Elke's eye. She knew something, and she thought I did, too. But she was wrong. I coughed and pointed to the hill behind the ridge. Under the orange-brown smoke cloud was a thin line of blazing brightness. The wildfire was moving higher.

"If the wind keeps going this way, it's going to make it over the hill. Time to go," I said.

We ran. Natasha stumbled, so we dragged her along between us. Sirens wailed ahead. The road had to be close. And suddenly there was the Prius. We almost ran right past it.

"At least no one stole it!" Elke pointed out.

I guess sometimes it's good to have an old, gray car. I bent over it, catching my breath while Elke looked inside the windows.

Natasha slumped against it. "Finally!"

"Yep." Elke squeezed Natasha's shoulder. "Can you unlock it?"

Natasha nodded and passed Elke the key from her pocket. "Do you want to drive?"

"Um, actually, I never learned!" Elke rolled her eyes. "I know, I know, but I never quite got around to it."

Natasha and I shared a stunned look.

"Seriously? I better do it then." Butterflies fluttered in my stomach. I'd only passed on the fourth go. Driving was definitely not my thing, but needs must, as Gran would say.

The click of unlocking filled the air. A reminder of how remote we were. Some of the contents of my bag spilled as Natasha opened the back door—my empty wallet, notebook and pencil, and my Oak Canyon College visitor's folder—from what seemed like another world and time. The past, present, and future were colliding.

Natasha stared at the Prius. It was covered in a film of ash. "My mom's gonna kill me." She took a big breath. "We don't even know where we are." She winced as she tried to climb in the back. Her eyes were dark shadows, her lips pale, and mascara smudged her cheeks.

"It's bad," I agreed. "None of us could have known how wild this night would get." My stomach squirmed even as I said it.

"No," said Elke. "Just like that Yosemite campfire night."

My whole body buzzed. *No, no, no, no, no, no, no.*

"That awful night," said Natasha. "I don't want to think about it anymore. I just want to get out of here and find Darius."

God, Darius, I hadn't even thought about him. "Yes, let's do that." I started the engine. "Here we go." I slipped the car into reverse, made a very sloppy eleven-point turn, and finally drove back down the fire road we'd come in on. My red-ringed eyes judged me in the rearview mirror.

I sped up, bumping the car along the rutted road. The headlight beams made an eerie glowing path through the thick haze. Trees shook their black branches at us as we passed, and small stones threw themselves at the wheels, doing their best to puncture them.

I just had to follow this road. It didn't even matter where we were, as long as we hit a main road. We'd be okay. The wildfire might be moving in our direction, but we could still easily drive out of danger. We'd find Darius, get Natasha's foot seen to, get back to the freeway, and get on with our lives. And I would never have to revisit campfire night again. But it was already too late. The memories were creeping back, no matter how hard I tried to lock them out.

DAWN

25

A SIREN CAME FROM DOWN IN THE VALLEY, WINDING ITS way up the mountain, rapidly followed by two more. Smoke wafted between the trees. I flicked on the windshield wipers to wipe away the fine ash layer, but it just smeared all over the windshield. Adding washer diluted it, but a layer of gray sludge remained.

"Keep going. We'll wash it properly when we get to a gas station," said Elke. "Can you see where you are?"

"Just about." I leaned in closer, squinting at the not-quite night, not-quite dawn light, as if that would help. The ruts in the road made for a bumpy ride.

"Can you try not to jolt so much?" Natasha spoke through clenched teeth. Her leg must be killing her.

"Sorry, sorry." I caught her face in the mirror. "Seriously, we'll get out of this."

She nodded but I knew she didn't really believe me. I'm not sure I did either. Creatures scurried across the road, two rabbits, a family of quails, even a deer. Racing away from the smoke. Every other moment I had to slam on the brakes, so as not to hit them, and at one point there was a horrible crunching sound as I hit a zigzagging squirrel.

"My God, Lily." Natasha turned around to see it. "It's limping!"

I was too busy trying not to gag to answer.

"What do you want her to do, slow down?" Elke asked.

Thank God we were going home. The wind had gotten stronger, and thick brown smoke wafted above the trees. It was so hot in the car with the windows up to stop the smoke coming in. My heart thumped and my head throbbed. I swallowed to stop my throat closing.

Elke kept watch behind. "No flames cresting the top of the hill yet. I don't see much more than the smoke. The wind is kicking up." She tutted. "I'm so glad we can drive out of this."

"God, me too." I looked in the rearview mirror. Big mistake, the glow behind the hill was like a sunrise, if the sun was huge and blazing. Right now, it was just a glow, but it was spreading across the sky. My hand trembled on the wheel. This was bad.

"Shit, you saw it," Elke shrugged. "I didn't want to distract you. We'll be fine. Just keep driving and get us to the main road."

Right, like I was trying to do anything else. I didn't bother to reply.

"You're doing great, Lily." Natasha tapped my shoulder. This tiny piece of encouragement from Natasha made me tear up. We had come so far. Probably still ten hours to go. If we made it. I smiled to myself. Middle school Lily would never have believed that all I wanted to do right then was drive ten hours home to safety with Elke and Natasha.

A swirl of leaves twirled across the road and a branch hit the front windshield. I ducked, then had to do a rapid course correction to avoid steering us into a ditch.

"I'm really thirsty," Natasha moaned. "We should have brought more water."

"What makes you think we didn't?" asked Elke, and she pulled out a water bottle from her backpack and passed it to Natasha. "Don't drink it all, save some for the rest of us."

Natasha nodded and gulped at the same time. Drips ran down her chin. When Elke handed it back to me, I drank it down greedily.

"Hey, slow down, I'm thirsty too!" Elke snatched it from me, but she was grinning.

"God," said Natasha, "I can't wait to get back to civilization."

Then we'd all go back to our previous personas: diva, daughter of a dying mother, and the faux "dropping" expert. I sighed to myself.

"What?" Natasha asked. "I thought you wanted to get back."

"I do. I do," and then I realized while I wanted to get us back safely, there was nothing to look forward to, just Mom's results. And they were "not what we hoped for." But she needed me, and I was not going to let her face the bad news alone. "Hey, Elke, see if you can find an emergency channel on the radio so we can find out what's going on."

"Oh, good idea!" She moved the dial painfully slowly to separate the static from anything that might be information.

Mandatory evacuations are underway for the area from west White Pine Mountain to Ravensdale. The storm winds are causing wildfire to move very rapidly in the area. People are advised not to wait but to evacuate immediately. Areas to the south and east should stand by for evacuation.

"Wow, that's that then." Elke arched her brows. "We're in the thick of it now."

"Shit!" Natasha called from the back seat. "This is the worst."

"We're going to be fine. We can't see the flames yet." I said, probably because they're hidden behind the smoke.

"God, I never thought we'd be in this situation again." Natasha's voice wavered.

"We aren't," said Elke, looking out the rear window. "We're not frightened, naive tweens anymore. We know what to do."

"We do?" I glanced at her. She was so calm. My whole body was trembling. I was just about keeping it inside my skin.

"Sure, we do. We're lucky we've been through this before. We know what to do—get away from the smoke as fast as possible, before the flames catch up, and don't wait for help."

"So, the equivalent of run?" I asked.

"And don't make a bad situation worse," she added, throwing me a do-you-get-me-look. "It's the good thing about learning from your mistakes, like I'd never make an illegal campfire now."

"Too right," said Natasha, "and I'd never put vodka in a Gatorade bottle and make Elke say it was hers."

"You're kidding!"

"I let her," said Elke, "so it was still my fault."

"Wow." Mind blown. I glanced in the rearview mirror. Big mistake. The glow had spread like a bloody sunrise.

"You've got this, Lily." Natasha cheered me on.

If only she knew. I bit my lip so bad it bled. My hands gripped the steering wheel. Thank God, I had something else to focus on, so I couldn't remember, couldn't see that whole night flash before me, couldn't relive what I had done.

Driving them out of this fire zone was the least I could do. I saw my face in the mirror, the same blue-green eyes, the same wide-eyed stare. The ghost of Lily past lay just beneath my skin.

"Look at that!" Natasha stared out the side window.

A haze of orange-brown smoke billowed across the sky.

Elke sniffed the air. "That smoke's getting much worse. Is it just me, or are we heading right toward it?"

"How can we be? The fire's behind us." I glanced in the rearview mirror just to be sure.

"Oh God, there must be two of them." Natasha looked back up at the orange glow coming off the mountain. "We're going to be trapped in the middle. There's no way out!"

"There are probably a few fires with that much lightning. But this road's still clear. I can get us out before the flames come. Hold on!" And I floored the accelerator, which on a Prius is not very dramatic. Every time I looked in the mirror, the blazing glow had spread.

Elke nodded. "I've got signal!" She pulled up her TRX app. "The main road is just ahead. No more than a mile, five more minutes. If we keep up this pace. We'll be fine."

I had no idea if the road was clear. I just had to believe it and make Natasha and Elke believe it. We had to make it. There was no other option.

The gas warning beeped. "Shit," I gasped.

"What?" asked Natasha.

"Gas," I said. No point in lying.

We bounced along, skidding on the dry dirt road.

Elke leaned over to check it. "Easy one mile left." Like she knew all about cars. "We'll be fine," Elke assured us.

"We'll be *fine*. That's your catchphrase. Everything will be fine. We won't be *fine* if we get stranded out here with no gas." Natasha's words came out in tight staccato bullets. "Slow down, Lily, or the gas won't last!"

Whoa. Both of their faces were rigid. They were going to explode. It was just a matter of who first.

I glanced back in the rearview mirror again and wished I hadn't. We'd made progress, but that fiery glow had rippling edges. It was smoky, hot, and airless. I coughed. My eyes watered with the effort of not going into a coughing fit. The wind was wild, shaking the trees, throwing up dirt like mini tornadoes. It would only take another spark to start a spot fire.

I glided the Prius along as far as possible without using more gas. "Come on, come on. Don't give up. The freeway can't be much farther," I said it like a plea, leaning in and rocking, like my pathetic motion would move it forward. If only we could be propelled by my hope, we'd be there by now.

Natasha shook her head. "We're running on fumes. We're never going to make it."

The car shuddered and came to a slow, agonizing halt.

26

"WHAT WERE YOU SAYING ABOUT GAS?" NATASHA MIGHT as well have slapped Elke.

"Are you seriously going to score points right now?" Elke snarled back.

"Stop. We've got to leave the car and run for the main road. No time to argue. All forgiven, remember?" I got out the car and begged them, "*Please*, let's just go."

Natasha clambered out, hiking sticks in hand. The wind whipped her skirt, revealing her purple bruised shin. She took a step, wobbled, and held her breath. "I'm sorry, I just…" She swallowed. "It hurts so much. You go on without me."

"No way," said Elke, their argument of two seconds ago lost in the wind. "We're not leaving you. We promised to stick together. So that's what we're doing."

Leaves and dust swirled in the air. The trees swayed right over with every new blast that battered them. It was like a storm without the rain. At least we'd made it out of the forest. Trees still lined the road, but they were less dense, and there was more open space behind them.

"Come on, Natasha, we've come so far, just keep going a little bit farther." I tried to grab her arm, but she shook her head. "Come on, you can do this." I tried to keep the irritation from my voice, but we were losing time.

"I can't and it doesn't make sense for one of us to damn the rest." Natasha leaned against the car. "I'll stay here. You go and get help."

We were frayed and afraid. I coughed as the smoke crawled into my lungs. The whole place stank, and the smoke was making it harder to see the road ahead—like a thick sepia fog hovering over everything.

"We're not leaving you." Elke covered her face with her T-shirt. "Leave the hazard lights on, maybe someone will see them and know we're close by."

I clicked them on. We left the doors wide open and hoped for the best. Natasha held on to her hiking sticks. We walked slowly but steadily, trying not to speed up too fast, and not to cringe every time Natasha tripped, slipped, or squealed in pain. It was awful.

"Let's hold up our phone lights so anyone who might be looking for evacuees can see us coming." They'd jiggle like fireflies and probably would be far too small to be seen, but anything to give a bit of hope. We were still way ahead of any flames.

"Good idea." Elke held hers up. It was way brighter than mine, but I held my phone up anyway. I wouldn't have any power left to call Mom if I ever got a signal again.

Every time Elke or I tried to help Natasha, she shook her head, planted her sticks, and swung her leg. Thank God for those sticks. Perhaps Neil wasn't a bad guy after all.

Between Natasha's leg and our sleep-deprived, anxiety-ridden state, we were so slow, it felt like we were crawling out of there. Every time we tried to speed it up, Natasha huffed deeper with the effort of constantly hopping. Sweat beaded on her forehead. The sticks helped and so did our support but still, it was exhausting. We weren't going to get through this.

Elke pointed out to the next landmark to head for, tree to rock, to fence post. It reminded me how I used to survive long-distance running, tricking myself that if I could just run to that far-off point, I could stop, but then adding one more point to aim for. I'd make the ten miles, one small goal at a time. Maybe that's how we should handle getting out of here. Just get to the road, then hitch a ride, then get to the freeway, then drive home. Just ten more hours to go. I took a deep sigh, almost wheezing as my lungs filled with smoke.

"What is it?" Elke asked.

I blinked back the tears and tried to catch my breath.

"Oh, you just realized when this is over, it's still not over." Elke grinned. How could she be grinning at a time like this?

I nodded. "When this bit's over, there are still hours before we get home."

"True," said Elke, "but let's worry about the drive home when we get to it."

I appreciated her trying to cheer me up, but I felt like I had suddenly gained fifty pounds, weighed down with the hopelessness of it all.

"At least you're not going to be killed for trashing your new car," said Natasha.

"New?" Elke and I said together.

"To me," said Natasha indignantly.

I glanced at Elke and couldn't stop it—a tiny giggle escaped my lips. Her shoulders jiggled. I tried so hard not to look at her. Tried so hard to keep the rising laughter under control.

"What's wrong with my car?" Natasha asked.

Elke and I couldn't contain it anymore. We laughed until tears ran down our cheeks. The more indignant Natasha got, the more we laughed. It wasn't until I was completely breathless that I finally managed to stop.

"I don't get it," said Natasha. "I thought you loved my car."

"We do," I said, and felt the giggles rising again.

"It is kind of shitty, isn't it?" said Natasha and she smiled, and her smile turned into a laugh, and within two seconds we were all laughing together, like we were back at middle school. Before all the bad stuff happened, and maybe this is what it could have been like.

"Oh my God, I'm going to wet myself," said Natasha. "No, no, seriously, stop." She wiped her eyes. "Oh, I needed that."

"I think we all did," said Elke. Then coughed. "We so have to get out of here." Understatement of the year.

The glowing sky had turned lava orange. Wind swirled the dirt into mini tornadoes.

Elke stopped and tilted her head. "Can you hear that?"

I listened. It sounded like a freight train coming closer. But I don't think she meant that. Then I heard it—a murmur, faint but there, an engine and way off in the distance, the tinny scream of an emergency siren.

"The main road!" Elke yelled. "We are so close!" She started running.

Natasha almost stopped. Every painful move was reflected in her face. Her eyes fluttered; her skin was clammy. I grasped her arm. She gave a tiny smile that was more like a goodbye and pushed me off. "You go," she whispered.

"No way, I'm not leaving you. And in case I never get to say it again. I am sorry that Elke left. And for everything I did that hurt you back then." *Whoosh*, that was a relief.

Natasha squeezed my hand. "I'm sorry, too. I was a bit of a shit back then," and she laughed at herself.

"You were, and still are a little, but so am I." And she didn't know the worst of it.

"But we're trying," said Natasha, "and that's how we grow."

I teared up. She was the last person I expected to hear that from.

"Come on!" Elke called to us. "I can almost see it!"

"Like she said." Natasha held out her arm. "Let's go." And I gratefully accepted it.

The flashing beams of the Prius were still visible behind us but only just. It would take a miracle for anyone to see them. I held my phone higher like that would help anyone see the faint flashlight beam. Another siren screamed much closer by.

I looked back and wished I hadn't. At the top of the mountain, we'd just come down, was a flickering ribbon of flame. The wildfire had spread, and the wind was pushing it toward us.

We were so close, but it didn't matter if you were only going a few steps at a time. There was no way we were going to outrun this situation.

"It's okay, you can still make it," said Natasha. Tears streamed down her face.

I shook my head. No way was I leaving her.

"Hey!" Elke called back to us. "Hear that?"

There was a rumble, racing toward us. We were trapped. My mind screamed, *Fire!* My guts yelled, *Run!* But the sound was all around us, circling in the smoke. And then nothing.

And there through the smoke, a vision appeared. It was Darius on his big, red, stupid motorcycle.

27

HE LEAPT OFF HIS MOTORCYCLE, LETTING IT CRASH ONTO
its side, and swooped Natasha awkwardly up in his arms. "I'm so
sorry. I'm so sorry. I've been looking for you for ages."

Natasha collapsed against his chest.

"I saw the lights, jiggling in the smoke." He laughed with relief.

"You noticed." Natasha threw her arms around his neck.

"I am sorry for taking so long. It was terrible. I got to the diner
and heard the evacuation warning, and I've been out here looking
for you guys ever since. Everyone's packed up and fleeing. I found
your car and you weren't with it. I've been driving up and down
the roads, and all around the trails, and there's so much smoke."
He paused, blinking back tears from his eyes. "I've finally found
you. And I brought the gas." He pointed to the orange canister and
laughed. "But you can't make it out of here in that car. There's a
fallen tree over the road behind me. I could barely get around it
on the bike. Branches are dropping everywhere." He stopped to
cough.

Natasha looked up at him. "Thank you."

He nodded and held her even tighter. "Of course. Where the hell were you?"

"We got lost in the woods, and I fell, and there was a stone ruin, and an old man." Natasha stopped. "It was awful."

I frowned at Darius. "Were you down by that old stone house?" I remembered when we were inside and I heard the rumble but thought it was thunder.

"That place? You were there? Oh, shit! I didn't see any movement. I thought it was empty." He looked horrified.

"Great," said Elke. "You're here now and we've gotta go!" She looked at the motorcycle. There was no way we were all getting out on that.

The plume of orange-brown smoke hovered right above us. Bright-orange flames flickered down the mountain, torching trees and turning them into matchsticks.

"We can beat it," said Darius. "The road runs away from the fire's direction. We just need to get to it. Then get you a ride, and we'll be totally out of here."

I wished I believed him, but I couldn't stop looking at those flames jumping and dancing down the hill, devouring everything in their path. They had to be easily a mile away, but they moved so fast.

Darius followed my gaze. "Trust me, we can make it."

There is something about the words *trust me* that fill me with dread, but I gave a fake smile. Then choked as I swallowed and coughed at the same time.

He wiped his sweaty forehead with the back of his hand. "I'm just…" He couldn't take his eyes off Natasha. "You won't believe how fucking relieved I am to find you." He wiped the sweat from his forehead. "Your foot, it looks bad."

"I kind of smashed it," said Natasha.

Darius picked his motorcycle up. "You guys need to run out of here. I'll take Natasha to the evacuation site, then come back for you, but don't wait for me. The only way out is through." He held out his arms to Natasha. "Come on, get on."

"Oh, my God. Oh, my God," murmured Natasha, as Elke and I helped her onto the motorcycle.

Elke leaned forward and grabbed her shoulders. "You've got this. We believe in you. We'll join you soon."

"We will." I nodded, like nodding manically would make it true. Mom flashed in my mind. What if I never saw her again, and she died not knowing what had happened? I swallowed down the tears that flooded my throat. "You can do this, Natasha. You have to."

"I feel terrible leaving you," Natasha called out.

"It's okay," Elke said. "We'll make it to the road and catch a ride. Go while you can." She squeezed Darius's shoulder. "Thank you."

"Of course! I'll come back for you once I get Natasha to safety. If I can. Follow the evacuation route, you can't miss it. Two wildfires coming toward each other, it's a mess out here! Okay, everyone, let's go!" Darius revved his engine. Natasha held tight to his waist, and away they went.

Elke grabbed my hand, and we ran after them.

The downed tree was easy to spot—a spruce that took up almost the entire width of the road. Its roots looked like wriggling fingers, newly exposed to the sky, and the trunk tapered away to an end point with almost no branches, as if they'd been stripped away by the wind.

"Wow," I murmured as we skirted around it. No wonder no cars had come by.

The brilliant glow on the ridge had spread across the whole sky. Fire trucks were on their way. I was sure of that. They'd take care of everything. We just had to get a ride to the evacuation site, then we'd be fine, too. Back to reality. Which, I realized, wasn't the same thing as fine at all. *Fine, fine, fine.* The word ricocheted around my head. The more I repeated it, the more absurd it sounded.

"Look at that!" Elke pointed up to the sky. A couple of hawks flew over followed by a flock of crows. "Where are they going?"

"Away from the fire?" I suggested.

Right then a rabbit ran across the road. It ignored us and continued loping down the hill.

"This feels like rats fleeing a sinking ship," I said. "We should go faster."

We sped up to a jog. Darius and Natasha had long since disappeared. It was hard running through the thick smoke. I held my T-shirt over my nose. My eyes were sore from fine, gritty ash, and I could hardly breathe. What if there was another fire ahead? "What if we're going the wrong way?" I didn't mean to blurt it out, but the thought was too loud to keep in my head.

"We're running the same direction as the animals. It has to be away from the fire," said Elke.

I could see why her mom didn't worry about her too much. "Another lesson learned at a dropping?" I asked.

Elke sighed. "I told you, I only did one once. They dropped us in the middle of a forest, like this, and left us for five hours to find our way out. I froze my butt off, went around in circles, got totally lost, didn't even make it out of the forest, and almost stepped in a bear trap. It was fucking terrifying." She stopped to get her breath back. "Got stung by nettles and laughed at by the other kids, cuz they were Dutch and had been before. They just wanted me to suffer. And that's when I decided I wasn't going to ever be unprepared again."

"I get that," I murmured. "But you're so confident. Like the expert on everything."

"I studied every how-to-survive guide and all the 'so you think you'd survive this' YouTube videos. I became so obsessed, Mom thought I was going to be a park ranger. I never realized what I needed was a 'how to survive middle school' guide." She glanced at me. "I think some of us don't survive as much as hide."

It was hard to breathe, and not just because of the smoke. She knew what I'd done for sure.

Images of that night at Yosemite swirled in my mind. It started with a spark, flying from the campfire. I watched it smolder on the ground until someone danced over it, extinguishing it. No one even noticed it existed, like they didn't notice me. I'd just wanted to pay them both back. That sounds so bad. It *was* so bad.

"It's easier to push the past away. I'm not the same person now." God, I hoped that was true.

"Are you not? I liked that Lily." Elke's boot steps punctuated each word.

"Maybe twelve-year-old Elke liked her. I'm not sure any of us would like her now."

Elke marched in silence for a while, and then turned to me and said, "But she's still part of you. Wherever you go, there you are."

"What, you quoting Dr. Seuss to me now?" I asked.

"It's from a mediation book, but you know what I mean."

I smiled but I knew Elke was right. No matter how hard I tried to push her away, tween Lily was still there. And being there with Elke and Natasha, in another fire situation, made it impossible to keep her hidden. She was right there with me. I could never get rid of her. And maybe that was, okay? "I'm truly sorry. I know I can't put it right. But I would if I could." I almost fell over, it was so hard to run, and think, and not cry.

"You can buy me a beer sometime," she said.

"Ha ha, if we ever get out of here."

We stayed lost in our own thoughts, our own regrets. I shivered in my flimsy hoodie, even as I sweated. My hand almost slipped from Elke's, but she gripped it tighter. I gave her a quick smile and we ran on.

28

"OH, IS THAT IT?" ELKE'S VOICE ROSE WITH EXCITEMENT as she pulled me along. "There it is!" She pointed to our right. The fire road we were running along finally met a paved two-lane road. We'd made it.

A siren pierced the air, followed by another. Their wails rose and fell with the wind and the curvature of the mountains as they sped along.

The plume behind us had turned orange-violet. The smoke was so thick, it blocked out the pale morning sun. You could see the particles of smoke in the air, brushing everything sepia.

It was early morning, but the heavy silence, with no birds, no voices, and that eerie light made it seem surreal. Unreal.

The sirens seemed like a good sign, but they'd faded away. I coughed. My ribs would crack trying to get any oxygen into my lungs. I slipped my T-shirt back over my nose.

"Wait," said Elke, and ripped off a strip from the bottom of her T-shirt. "I'm warm enough." She tore it in half and passed me a piece. We made light work of fixing them into face masks. It was hot and sweaty, but better than breathing in all that gunk.

A white pickup truck with massive wheels rushed by, forcing us back into the brambles. A thorn scraped across my arm, leaving a trail of red beads where it broke my skin. I ignored it and carried on running behind Elke.

"We'll get to the nearest emergency services. They'll help. They have to, right?" I asked.

"If they're not fighting fires, maybe," said Elke.

The smoke became almost overpowering. It was a new kind, acrid, with a burned-tire undertone. Like several fires merging their toxic smoke. *Shit.*

The road went downhill, which was good, but there still weren't many cars, which was bad. The trees were farther back from the road, and the area was dotted with fields and occasional barns. We were moving closer to civilization and that had to mean help and safety.

"Darius said the evacuation place wasn't far, right?" *Right? Please be right!* I looked at Elke for confirmation.

"Don't worry, we're doing all we can." She gave a faint smile like that would make me feel better. Racing between fires was all we could do, and it wasn't enough.

Finally, an engine noise rumbled toward us. We walked backward and stuck out our thumbs. A cobalt-blue SUV, with three children's faces squashed against the windows, zoomed by. One of them waved and smiled. Moments later, another dirty white pickup passed by, packed with crates of oranges in the back. It was more vehicles than we'd seen the whole night. But they all sped on like they didn't see us at all.

Elke jumped into the road and stuck out both thumbs at the sound of the next engine.

A deep-purple pickup truck rolled by. The driver yelled out the window. "Get out of the road!" Like we wanted to be walking in this hell.

There was no way we were getting a ride. A fire truck sped by, spinning red and white lights.

"Oh, my God, stop and give us a ride, PLEASE!" Elke yelled.

"They didn't even see us." I watched them disappear back up the road.

The wind whipped up. I swear there was a crackling in the distance. The rising sun highlighted the smoke smothering everything in a thick, glowing deep orange. It was everywhere, a totally burned sky. There was no way these fires weren't worth freaking out about. The edges of everything blurred in the smoke.

"We'd better pray we get a ride." I glanced down the deserted road, then up to the glowing sky. It was like a movie set. A movie set in hell. I held out my hand and a pattering of thick ash fell on it.

"Come on, speed up!" Elke demanded.

I jogged after her, but we were just sucking in the smoke particles. "Stop," I bent over to get a breath. "Running makes the breathing worse."

"Okay, Doctor Lily, how else are we supposed to get out of here?"

"I don't know," I admitted. "Do you think Darius will come back for us?"

"Who knows? I have a feeling he won't want to leave Natasha's side, like ever again."

"She looked so relieved to see him." I stared wistfully down the road. "It must feel amazing to know someone cared about you so much they literally risked their life for you."

"Seriously, Lily, are you getting all romantic on me, now?" Elke grinned.

I shook my head, "No, I'm just saying, it must be nice."

"Yes." She nodded. "Come on, we can't stop. We'll see them both soon."

"This is wrong." I looked around us, and it was hard to tell what anything was. The wind must have changed. The smoke was so thick that we could be walking through a field, and I wouldn't know.

"Only way out is through," Elke yelled back. "Grab my hand!"

I did and we ran for what seemed like an eternity but was probably only ten minutes—ten minutes with the smoke getting thicker. We slowed down to a walk when we could hear the sound of more vehicles, at first a truck and then maybe a motorcycle, and we knew we had to be close to that junction.

"How far do you think?"

Elke shrugged. "No idea. Guess we'd better keep walking."

"It's so strange, the three of us back together again in a fire situation, like some kind of divine retribution." I hadn't meant to say that out loud.

"Wrong place, wrong time," said Elke matter-of-factly. "Don't let it get to you. It's a random act of coincidence. Unlike the fire."

My stomach felt hollow and bottomless. "I didn't mean it to go that far at Yosemite camp."

Elke nodded. "I know."

And then another memory: her eyes meeting mine that night. Under the cover of darkness. We had both stared at each other for a split second, before I gathered my wits and shouted, *"FIRE! FIRE!"* like I was trying to save everyone. Which I totally was.

We hadn't seen each other at all after that. Not until this trip. She'd disappeared in the haze of eighth grade, and I'd never even heard what happened to her. I guess it didn't help that Natasha and I weren't friends anymore either. "I'm sorry I never got to apologize at the time."

Elke shrugged. "You couldn't help that. But thank you for caring." She glanced at me. "You're here with me. That's what counts. Who you are now."

I nodded, and we ran on a bit in silence. The wind shifted, making the smoke drift apart so we could see the road, at least six feet ahead. We were still on track to the evacuation site.

We slowed down a little, and Elke picked up the conversation again. "Ever since it happened, Natasha wanted to get back at you. At first, I wanted it too, but DC kind of turned out better." Elke flipped a stray strand of violet hair from her eyes. "It was eighth grade. We were all trying to find ourselves." She sighed. "I was going through a lot, with my dad dying and being back where it happened." She shook her head. "The campfire isn't the thing that haunts me."

"Why are you being so nice to me?" I asked.

Elke smiled. "I'm not. I'm just saying it was what it was. We're all just trying, and it's not like we're going to hang out after this, so why not clear the air while we can?"

Right then, I was saddened by the thought that we'd never speak to each other again, but I knew she was right. Why would we? We moved in completely different circles. We wouldn't go to the same college, so why would we ever contact each other again?

I nodded and wiped the tears away. "Twelve-year-old Lily was awful."

"Twelve-year-old Lily was fun and interesting. She did one stupid thing that she deeply regrets, that's all. Apology accepted." Elke smiled, and her green eyes lit up. "Seriously, I'm giving you a second chance. Take it."

I hugged her. And she hugged me back.

"Come on then," she said, and we ran on together toward the rumbling as it grew louder and louder. It was the impatient sound of slow-moving traffic.

There was no way we wouldn't get a ride. The joy I felt was reflected in the look on Elke's face. We were getting out of here.

29

"WAY, HEY, HEY, LADIES!" A SOFT-TOP JEEP PULLED alongside us. Three frat boys leered out the windows.

Of course, that would be the first offer. I shook my head and walked quickly on, linking my arm with Elke's. It was a crap vehicle to escape a fire in anyway.

"You'll regret that!" they yelled as they pulled away.

"I doubt it!" I yelled back before Elke could.

She gave me a huge grin. "You tell them!"

A mud-splattered black truck rolled by followed by the brightest aqua-blue sports car. They didn't slow down. Another car came toward us, a MINI stuffed to the brim with students. It was unreal that so many people had been out here the whole time. The area had seemed so remote, so unpopulated. I guess some farms are easier to spot than others hidden way back from the road, and some inhabitants, like Old Neil and the RV woman, go out of their way to stay invisible.

Thank God, we'd found our way out of the forest and onto the road.

"Has to be this way, right?" I asked.

Elke nodded, looking up the winding road to her right, then down to the left where everyone seemed to be headed. "Maybe there was an announcement or something we missed, like when they send out an early earthquake warning."

"We wouldn't have got it with no cell signal anyway. Downhill is easier to run than uphill. So let's hope they're right!"

We jogged down the road after them. A couple more cars zoomed by.

Elke and I exchanged a glance. I really thought it would be easier than this.

"Do you think Darius won't come back for us?" I swallowed.

"Of course, if he will, if he can," Elke assured me. "But we'll find a ride. Not everyone can ignore us."

A Tesla driver honked his horn as he sped by us. Classy.

"Shit, we're never getting out of here." I coughed. It was too painful to run now. Smoke billowed across the sky like a thick burnt-orange blanket. The flames wouldn't be far behind.

I glanced inside the cars as I followed Elke down the road. Trying to spot a kind stranger with two spare seats was hard. Mostly they refused to meet my eyes, or shrugged and looked sad for me, but not sad enough to squeeze us in. The ashy snow left a film of gray across the vehicles and in our hair.

Elke raised her brows. "Out of the frying pan into the fire!"

I knew she was trying to make light of the situation, but it was a little too close to the bone. She wrinkled her nose. "It's a bit scary, but there was at least one police car."

"But going the other way."

212

Elke continued. "And look, a helicopter!" She pointed above as one flew over us and away toward the mountain. "How bad can it be?"

"Bad. Remember last year when we almost got evacuated and had to pack everything and be ready to run, just in case?" I asked.

"Nope, I was in DC," she answered.

"There were helicopters and planes dropping retardant. The school was closed because of the potential evacuation, and the smoke was too bad to go outside. The gas stations were out of gas, and everyone was panic buying bottles of water, because any minute we might have to drive for our lives. We were lucky. Some towns got completely razed by wildfire."

"Okay, I get it." Elke stuck her thumb out. "Come on, let's shame these people into giving us a ride before the same thing happens here."

I looked back at where we'd come from. Sparks whirled high up in the air. They were at least two thousand feet away, but still sparks! It wouldn't take much for a gust of wind to blow them farther down to the road. Dark-gray smoke clouds gathered ahead of us, and the thick orange smoke above the mountain reached out to meet them. At this rate, two wildfires were going to become one fast.

"It's catching up with us!" I couldn't keep the edge of panic from my voice.

A Mercedes beeped repeatedly as it glided by, as if to tell us to get out of the road.

"Oh my *God*, calm down!" Elke yelled, not sounded calm at all. "Thanks for nothing!" she yelled after him, as if he could hear anything in his world-proof Mercedes bubble.

That driver's anger started off a cascade of beeping horns. I watched the family next to us, stuck in their car. There were two kids, twins I'd guess, with their faces pressed against the window, along with a little foot. I waved. They waved back and made goofy faces, until their parents told them off and frowned at me for making faces back. No ride was offered.

The wind was wild, tossing trees from side to side. A branch fell right in front of us. And a whole tree just behind it.

"Jesus!" I pointed at them. "We're going to die out here."

"Would you rather be burned to death or brained?" asked Elke, rummaging in her backpack. "Water?"

"Ah, neither thanks." I took the steel bottle from her. Anything to keep my mind off what was happening out there. "Goddammit, give us a ride!" I yelled.

Elke shook her head, "No one's going to pick you up if you're growling!" Sweat beaded on her upper lip.

"It's hopeless. We should have gone with the frat guys!" I coughed into my T-shirt.

Elke turned to laugh and almost got smashed into by a RAV4 trying to jump the line. "What the hell!" She hit the roof as the car swerved back onto the road.

"Jesus, Elke." It was hard to see if there was anyone inside through the blacked-out windows. "They could have had a gun or anything."

"What? They almost crashed into me!"

"It's a tense situation!" I practically shouted. "And you're not helping."

The air swirled with ash, raining down on the car like snow. It wouldn't take long before the wildfire would reach the road.

There was a short row of red lights ahead of us through the smoke as every vehicle we'd just seen stopped, then slowly moved forward, then stopped again. Everyone honked their horns. The air was tense with fear. My whole body bounced with adrenaline.

"Where did they all even come from?" I asked. "I mean, I know people live out here but this many?"

"The evacuation must be wide. No need to really worry until we see the flames much closer," said Elke. "We can easily outrun this." By now I had serious doubts about her survival skills.

"And then when the flames do catch up to us, what? We just run faster?" I snapped. Shit, I shouldn't have said anything. "Sorry."

Elke gripped my hand. "It's scary. I'm scared, too."

A car had stopped on the other side of the road. Everyone turned to look at it as they passed. A guy was trying to change a tire. I felt bad that we didn't stop to help, but what could we have done? Lend him our nonworking phones?

"Hey, need a ride?" A guy with a bright-red sunburned nose poked his head out the window of a white pickup truck.

His passenger, a slightly older guy, grinned at us and nodded. Jesus, we'd stopped even bothering to hitch. It had to be better than waiting for the frat guys to catch up to us.

"A ride?" the driver repeated. "We've got room."

I kept my T-shirt over my mouth and glanced at Elke, masked and ashen-faced.

"It's okay, we don't bite." The older guy added. His brown eyes seemed friendly, concerned, just trying to help.

I raised my brows at Elke. "What do you think?" Jumping in a truck with two guys was reckless in normal times, but the fire was gaining on us, and it could be our last chance to escape.

Elke couldn't seem to focus. Her eyes switched from me to the guy to the fire behind us in quick succession.

"It's getting pretty bad," the first guy yelled out the window. They were right. The smoke had become so thick, it wouldn't matter if we died out here from smoke inhalation, or got stranded and stuck, unable to leave before the flames reached us.

I made an executive decision. "Sure, thank you!" and grabbed Elke's hand. "It's our best shot," I assured her.

She blinked like she'd just come back to reality and piled with me into the back of the truck. I just hoped we hadn't caught a ride too late.

MORNING

30

THE SUNBURNED GUY LEANED BACK AND SMILED. "I'M glad you jumped in. I'd never have forgiven myself if you'd got stuck in that. I'm Chase and that's Ryan, by the way."

There was a long silence where we nodded and didn't give our names or pull off our masks. Because it's not like they needed to know anything about us.

"How come you were walking, anyway?" asked Chase.

"We got separated from our friends," said Elke.

"Ran out of gas," I added. As if Elke's story needed further explanation.

It didn't matter if they believed us or not. They'd picked us up and that was all that mattered.

"We'd kind of given up," I said, crossing and uncrossing my legs.

"Hey, no problem," said Chase. "This is a unusual situation. Never thought our weekend would end up like this."

"Us neither," Elke agreed. "Thanks anyway, for stopping for us."

"Of course," Ryan said. "What kind of people don't stop to help in a crisis?"

"Most," Elke and I said together.

I gave Elke a quick smile, and she gave a little nod back. Sweat dripped down my back, and I become very aware that we hadn't showered in a day and were covered in dusty mud and ash. I squirmed in my seat and checked my phone. Still no signal. I sighed heavier than I'd meant to.

"We were so freaked out getting that evacuation notice that we didn't know where to go. We're not from here, and we couldn't pack all our shit up fast enough. We finally got rooms in our favorite winery and just wanted to flee as soon as we saw that smoke. That smell! And then that beeping evacuation warning. I couldn't wait to get out of there. We left a crate of wine behind; no way was I going back for it. Where were you staying?" He was a full-on flood of oversharing. Nerves, I realized. He was as scared as we were.

Elke and I exchanged raised brows.

Chase carried on, "Airbnb? Campsite? Farm?"

"We stayed with friends." I said it like nothing had happened. There was no double prank, no getting lost, no stone house, no Old Neil, and no being chased by wildfire. My hands trembled.

Chase took the hint and stopped talking. He drove slowly along, past clumps of gossiping trees, occasional oversized barns, and a couple of farmhouses. A sign said Drain was ten miles away, and the I-5 freeway, thirteen miles. Thirteen miles—we could almost walk it!

Smoke blotted out the sun completely, covering the sky in a deep sienna glow. Ash rained on the windshield, changing into a gray pulp every time Chase tried to clean it off with the wipers.

"Oh my God. Oh my God," Ryan muttered to himself. "We're never going to get out of this." He looked so panicked.

Chase grabbed his hand. "We can do this."

But judging by the tense grip on the steering wheel, it seemed like Chase felt the same way.

"If we keep crawling like this, we're never going to make it," he finally said out loud.

A fire engine sped past going the other way, its siren slashing through the air.

My heart thrummed. The few cars ahead kept stopping and starting, and behind us the flames were racing along the edges of the road. Shit, Chase was right. The fire was moving quicker than the traffic. We were still an easy thousand feet away, but not for long.

The wind pushed against the truck. A power line fell in front of us, the electric cable whipping from side to side.

"Chase!" I yelled, just in time for him to swerve, avoiding it but almost crashing into a tree as he went up the grassy verge and down again.

The car behind us skidded to a complete stop. The car ahead sped up. Another siren shot by us. An ambulance, I think. My stomach was a roller coaster doing nonstop loops.

"Are we even going the right way?" Chase looked at the flashing lights receding into the smoke.

I lurched forward. "Can we go any faster?" It was a ridiculous question. We were trapped.

"It's okay. We're going to make it." Ryan's voice quivered. Sweat dripped down his cheek, not very reassuring.

Chase raised his brows at Ryan but didn't say anything. He fiddled with his baseball cap and kept glancing at the side-view mirror as if to check we weren't being followed, which would be hard in this slow-moving line. Unless you were on a motorcycle. Shivers prickled up my spine. Were Darius and Natasha okay? I looked in the side-view mirror, hopeful I'd catch sight of the bright-red bike.

"Do you want some water?" Ryan shook his water bottle at us.

"That would be great," said Elke. She took it from him and chugged it down.

"I'm fine, but thank you," I said. I was so far from being fine.

The car was hot and getting hotter. Even my door handle was hot. An explosion sounded in the distance, then another, closer. I startled and looked wildly behind us.

"Propane tanks?" Elke asked.

"Must be, like Old Neil had warned us."

"Old Neil?" Ryan asked.

"No one," I said.

"Just a guy we met," Elke said at the same time.

A guy that we ran from. Was he really chasing us though? Whatever, I hoped he and Hunter had gotten away from the fire. No one deserves to be trapped in that.

We slowed right down again. The car behind honked their horn. There was a crackling sound, like fireworks spitting as they launch. A field flickered with fire like a glowing meadow. The whole sky was bright blazing orange. No pretense this was ever going to be a regular day.

"It's okay, we'll get you out of here," Ryan said, with sweat pouring down his face. "Don't worry."

Don't worry is what doctors say when they know the odds are against you. Don't worry, plenty of people survive cancer. But plenty do not. And it didn't depend on how hard you fought. It depended on how severe the cancer was. It was luck. Or lack of it. *Not the results we'd hoped for.* We were all here in this truck down to luck.

I checked my phone again. Oh, Mom, I am trying so hard to get back to you. I took a deep breath. It was seven o'clock and there was no sun, only an eerie orange glow, as if this whole place was under its own dome.

I started coughing, great hacking, lung-aching coughs. The smoke was so thick. Ryan passed me the water and I took a swig.

I glanced behind us. Big mistake. The wildfire was moving like lava down the mountain. Flames flickered their way through the surrounding forest and danced along the surrounding fields. Waves of flames climbed higher, and higher, leaping from tree to tree, rippling along like the fire was running after us.

"Drive faster!" I yelled.

Elke and Ryan turned to look back, too.

"Shit, we're not going to make it." And for the first time, Elke actually looked scared.

"We're all going to make it, trust me." Ryan nodded at Chase. "Right?"

He didn't look so sure. The flames exploded through the trees, racing ever closer to the road. Sparks flew ahead on the wind, catching fire immediately as they landed on the dry grass, in the tinderbox that was rural Oregon.

"I've never seen a fire move this fast," said Chase, honking the horn, as if that was going to help.

Ryan leaned forward. "I'll jump out and see what's holding us up."
He opened the door. "Be right back."

"Always has to play the hero," Chase said, shaking his head. "You know he's shit scared right? It's just his way. He doesn't want me to see it. Like I wouldn't know."

We sat in silence. Every time I looked behind me, the flames were closer. I watched as a huge barn in the distance went up in flames in seconds. The whole structure glowed bright orange, like a giant fiery pumpkin. We were moving too slowly. We'd never make it out, stuck with all these nonmoving vehicles. We'd burn to death in them.

I texted Mom. Oh my God, we had a signal!

love you, delayed but fine, ten hours to go, love you

I didn't realize I'd done a double *love you* until I'd pressed Send, but what did it matter? I did double love her.

I shoved my phone back in my pocket. There was no way I could tell her the truth—stuck in traffic, likely to be burned to death, sorry for everything, bye forever.

I told Elke we had signal. But she shook her head. "Mom doesn't even know I'm here."

"Where does she think you are?" I whispered.

"With Sasha, staying in Portland." She shrugged. "She'll only worry."

Yes, for good reason. But Elke was right. No point in worrying people unless they needed for sure to be worried. It's not like they could do anything, anyway.

My thighs stuck to the seat, sweat dripped behind my knees, even my shins were sweating. It was so hot, so stuffy, so hard to breathe. Everything was coated in ash, everything was dying.

Ryan jumped back into the passenger seat. "There's a crash up ahead, across both lanes so it's tough to get by. We'll pass it soon." Chase was right; Ryan's whole body was trembling.

I wiped the sweat from my forehead. It was the smoke, the fire, and the sense of impending doom. We couldn't just sit there. We had to do something. Elke's leg bounced as she hid her hands in her jacket pockets. I swallowed back the rising bile. Chase opened, then closed the window. Ryan drummed on the dashboard until Chase slapped his hand. Everyone was on edge.

"Watch the road," Ryan yelled as we almost ran into a police car coming the other way.

We were crawling so slowly, but the smoke made it hard to see very far, and all it took was for Chase to lose focus for one second. I swallowed. We hadn't crashed. Yet.

The police car sped by, lights flashing, sirens wailing. All the emergency services were headed in the other direction. No one was stopping to help us get out of there.

Sparks scattered across the road. Streams of flames flickered behind them.

"We won't get through, and even if we do, we'll be heading into a firestorm." My voice faltered. "We should run."

"No, no. It's safer in the truck," Chase reassured me.

I caught Elke's eye. *Are you with me?* She nodded.

"You're right." Elke flung open the door. "We gotta run."

"Good luck and thank you!" I yelled as I scrabbled after her.

We raced along the road. Our eyes streamed. Sparks floated above our heads like fire dust. We held our T-shirts over our faces, to ineffectually protect us from the smoke, and ran as fast as we could toward safety. A fireball rolled in front of us, bursting onto the road. Sparks hit an abandoned truck and danced past our eyes.

The sky was dark as midnight—if midnight had an eerie orange glow to it. We could hardly see where we were running. A shape emerged ahead, the crashed car. The Tesla. It was completely crunched in at the front, with the side door ripped off. We were afraid to look inside. And there was no time to waste.

31

A SIREN WAILED AHEAD. "HEAD FOR THE SOUND," I shouted between coughs.

Every step hurt my lungs. I slowed down. Elke pulled me along, almost tipping me over, but I rebalanced and hauled myself forward. Embers jumped from tree to tree, coming ever closer, just like I'd feared. A tree burst into flames less than twenty feet away, exploding sparks everywhere. We looked at each other with wide eyes. Then we ran, racing for our lives.

"Keep going! Keep going!" I yelled.

A black SUV ahead had pulled over at the side of the road. Next to it, a guy held up his phone, trying to record the action. His wife was shouting at him from inside the car.

"Get out!" I yelled as we passed them. "The fire's coming!" As if they couldn't see the orange sky and the thick smoke around us.

They opened their car doors, grabbed their two kids, and ran. There was no way anyone was driving their way out of this mess. Sparks flickered right behind us, twirling like deadly fireflies. Elke and I hurtled each other along.

We reached the taillights of another stalled GMC truck. It was already empty. Doors left open, abandoned bags falling out. A steel water bottle rolled back and forth on the road, clattering like a death rattle. It didn't matter how big your wheels were, or how many people your car could seat, or what your bumper sticker said. In the end everyone was equally stuck.

"Keep running," Elke yelled. "Don't stop!" As if there was any chance I was slowing down.

We ran to the siren's sound, leaving the fire behind us. The fire truck took off just as we arrived.

"Keep going across the bridge!" a firefighter shouted out the window. I couldn't stop staring at the SEARCH AND RESCUE sign on her yellow overalls. She pointed down the road to where the bridge was. "Follow everyone else. Take these just in case!" She threw us a couple of silver foil blankets. "Stay away from the trees, and if the fire suddenly changes direction—and this is *really important*—lie on the ground, cover yourselves with these, and stay on the cement pavement."

I caught the blankets. Great. If in doubt, cover yourself in foil. I hoped to God we wouldn't need to. We ran-walked, weaving past the mom and dad, no longer arguing, carrying their tired children, and a couple of women running with their yellow Lab on a leash, all determinedly focused on the way ahead. Two hikers were ahead of them, with their bulky backpacks, carrying water bottles and hiking sticks. *Hiking sticks.* Which made me think of Natasha.

"Do you think Darius and Natasha will be waiting there for us?" I looked around wildly, as if they would be waiting at the side of the road for us.

"No." Elke glanced around, too. "Darius said he'd take her to the evacuation site."

"That has to be past the bridge." I waited for an answer, but Elke just nodded and hurried along. It was too hard to talk and breathe at the same time anyway.

We passed a couple of farms with clapboard farmhouses set back from the road. A few RVs were back in the trees with mud-grimed sides and rusty pickup trucks. Fire flickered along the woods, bright white at the base and blazing orange above. The flames rippled from tree to tree.

In the distance behind us, the fire had jumped across the road. Any cars over a thousand feet away were completely cut off. I clambered over a fallen branch. It was almost impossible for anyone to drive now anyway, with all the debris littering the road—chunks of burning branches, downed power lines, a melting garbage can.

Sparks swirled like fairy dust, mesmerizing in their brightness, as they rode on the wind, catching on dried-up vegetation and spreading ever closer to us.

Those sparks. A memory hit me like a punch in the gut. I doubled over. I squeezed my eyes closed as if that would stop it from coming back. The image I'd been running from ran right alongside me, refusing to be shut out anymore.

That night at the Yosemite camp, after the first spark from Elke's campfire flamed up and died without anyone noticing, I'd kicked out another ember. I'd watched it glow and grow, flicker across the dried grass and catch the tree. And when I looked back at the party, that's when Elke locked eyes with me.

She knew. I'd made the fire spread.

"You okay?" Elke asked, frowning with concern.

"It's nothing," And everything. My whole body trembled.

How had I done that? How had I not remembered that it was *me*? Elke knew and hadn't told anyone. The campfire disaster wasn't Natasha's fault, or Elke's. It was me, all me. And all this time I'd hidden it from myself. What kind of person does that? A terrible person.

I caught my breath and froze. The world swirled.

Elke stared at me, all soot-stained cheeks, and red-rimmed eyes. "You sure you're okay?"

I nodded, avoiding her eyes, and ran on beside her. I'd started it. I'd spread the Yosemite campfire. I kicked the ember and watched it burn and did nothing to stop it. I must have pushed the memory so far down, like a bad dream. But being there with Elke and Natasha had brought it all back.

I shook my head. How could I have done that? Was I hurting that badly? I couldn't remember. No, I could, I had to. My eyes were blurry with tears. At least Elke would think it was smoke. Did I really care? Anyway, she already knew. She was just waiting for me to confess.

I peeked at her. She was focused on the escape route ahead. I coughed and paused for a second to catch my breath before running on again. It took Elke a couple of seconds to notice, then she stopped and smiled at me. I fake smiled back.

I was wrong. I couldn't become someone new. My past was still there with me, attached like a shadow.

That fateful Yosemite camp week, we'd found out that Mom's cancer had come roaring back. Natasha, my so-called best friend, didn't even call me when I left the tearful voice message telling her the news. She was the only one who knew that Mom was sick. Obviously, Natasha didn't care anymore. It had already turned into the Natasha and Elke Best Friends Forever show.

I'd tried hiding the truth about my mom for so long, only to have it called over the school intercom. *Lily Williams to the counselor's office. Lily Williams.* I knew that had to mean bad news about Mom. Just remembering those words made my knees buckle. I took all the pain of rejection and fear and focused it on blaming Natasha and Elke.

Another explosion came right behind us. I ducked and we ran. Trees lit up and sparked like rows of candles. Smoke billowed above, smoldering the sky. A swirl of burning pine branches flew in front of me. Spot fires were burning everywhere. The wind blasted hard enough to pull us apart for a moment before we clung to each other again.

"I'm glad I got to say thank you. I was wrong about you. You're not who I thought you were." I panted with the effort of speaking and breathing at the same time in that thick smoke. *And I am not who I thought I was.*

"Not a Viking? The Dutch were never Vikings." Elke coughed and adjusted her homemade mask. "I used to hate how everyone at school got that wrong. Now it's just funny."

"I thought you were too cool, too interesting, too smart." I paused to catch my breath again. "I used to judge myself against you."

Elke slowed down. "It's easier to seem cool when you start somewhere new. But that's not the real me." She shook her head and jogged on, slower now. "I'm terrified if I stop running, time will catch up, and what if I die young like my dad?" She stopped so suddenly, I almost ran into her. She looked deep into my eyes. "If I stop, I remember, and"—she gulped—"then what? Who am I? It's like I don't know. I'm not here." She looked back at the wall of smoke and flames. "I don't want to die here."

We were all just scared. I hugged her and felt a tear slid down her cheek onto mine. "You said I never stand up for myself. Say yes when I mean no. But you always seem so brave."

"Fake it till you make it." She leaned up and kissed me on the cheek, "Thank you, Lily, for being here."

"Of course." She knew everything and she was still there for me. I grabbed her hand as we ran. Anyone would think we were besties.

We took off again, crossing the street, stepping around abandoned cars. We never were enemies. We were just middle graders doing our best to survive.

Elke blinked her jade-green eyes at me. "I know you like me, really, always have."

"I don't hate you now, and never have." I squeezed her hand and let it go.

"I know." She stopped running and placed her hand on my shoulder. "I get it." And Elke brushed a fleck of ash from my cheek and smiled. "Come on, let's get the hell out of here!"

And we were off again. Behind us, a looming orange blaze of smoke billowed, and flames shot into the sky. Every now and then something else exploded. Each of my breaths was punctuated by the sound of footsteps racing toward the evacuation point, a constant reminder that I was still alive, that I was here, with Elke.

32

A WHITE MARE RAN BY, CLOSELY FOLLOWED BY A GIRL
riding a black stallion, who seemed to be guiding them both. They
ran toward the bridge that appeared ahead.

It was a rickety wooden bridge, with two narrow lanes going
across it and tall railed sides.

I stopped at the entrance and shivered. There was no way this
would stand up to a fire.

"Come on. Keep going!" Elke begged me. "We're so close!"

"Right! Over the bridge and through the hills." My stomach
lurched, but I took Elke's outstretched hand, and we ran across that
bridge like two schoolkids, screaming and pretending to be fine
when we were actually scared to death.

The bridge shuddered as we ran. The river below was a sludgy
deep green and slow, shallow enough for rocks to make a stepping-
stone path across. I bet it was pretty when it wasn't surrounded by
smoke and fire and people fleeing for their lives. A few people gathered by the river's edge, waiting it out by the water. Maybe that's
what we should do. No, we needed to find Natasha and Darius. Our

feet echoed as we pounded along, followed by the women and their yellow Lab, catching up behind us. One of them stopped for a second, almost tripping me up.

"Gracie, Gracie, here, girl!" The dog leapt back to her owner. The woman gave me a how-did-we-get-here grimace before running on.

I looked around for Elke, spotting her violet hair ahead. She was looking back for me. I waved and she saw me and smiled. We ran to each other.

"Oh my God, for a second I thought I'd lost you," I said breathlessly.

"Same." Elke swallowed hard and coughed. "Okay?"

The bridge led to a crossroads. The road that went over the bridge continued straight ahead, and another small road cut across it, following the curve of the river. A row of vehicles was lined up on the smaller road behind a police car, engines revving, brake lights on, like they were waiting impatiently for the order to go.

The police car siren whooped. An officer shouted out, "Last chance, hurry, let's go!"

The family we'd seen before rushed to get a spot, banging on car doors, begging for a ride. A man hurried by me, shouting over his shoulder, "The police car's clearing a path for everyone to follow." He yanked open the last pick-up truck's door and squashed his way in.

Ah, so there was a way to drive out. If you were quick enough to grab a ride in a willing car. Which we weren't. They were desperate to leave, shouting out their windows and honking their horns.

"Let's go," the officer yelled. Their siren blazed as they headed off, slowly followed by the lucky vehicles behind it.

"Shit, that should have been us." We were just running, not thinking and figuring our way out. We couldn't just keep on running.

Elke looked at me, not seeming to understand what was happening. I urged her across the road. The fire hadn't got that far, but it was only a matter of time before it did. I glanced back at the bridge. It was barely five hundred feet away and already nothing but smoke and twisting flames, some thirty feet high. They raced through everything in their path, clutching at trees, sending ribbons of flickering fire dancing on the house roofs and down to the abandoned cars.

The houses were mirages of heat, glowing white and yellow, where windows and doors used to be, the insides reduced to hollow furnaces in seconds, and then nothing but twisted metal, scorched black walls, and white crumbling dust.

We scanned the road in silence, unsure what way to go. One fire was behind us and the other closing in from our right. Left and forward, the way the police car had gone. It was our only hope. At least for now the flames hadn't crossed over this road.

"Shit!" Elke stopped short and pointed to a blackened tree. There at the base of the twisted trunk was a crashed motorcycle.

We rushed to it. The handlebars and scorched wheels were still in place, and the metal frame of the seat, but the rear wheel was twisted and the seat cushion and tires had completely melted away.

"It might not be," I started. Elke's look silenced me.

She pointed to the singed red fuel tank. It had to be Darius's.

"How did they end up there?" It made no sense.

"Oh, Darius," Elke murmured. "Look, skid marks. He was

235

probably speeding, trying to escape, and then crashed right into the path of a fire."

She was right. There were spot fires erupting everywhere as sparks flew up in the wind and settled on the dry vegetation. I bent down to inspect the wreckage. The whole bike was twisted out of shape, like a giant metal insect, covered in soot with piles of gray ash all around it.

"I can't look." Elke slumped to the ground. "Darius must have been trying to get Natasha to safety, and then the flames..." She stopped talking and shook her head. Tears streamed down her face. "It was my fault. I told him to come back for us. What am I going to tell Natasha's mom?" Elke let out a little wail. "What am I going to tell Sasha?"

My heart plummeted. "They might be okay. Anything could have happened. And they're not here. And there's no blood. That's a good thing." I hoped it was a good thing.

"Anything could have happened," she mimicked me. "Including they're dead." She looked up at me. "This is all my fault. I should have stopped Natasha from giving you a ride. I should have stayed with Sasha. I could have done something. Stopped the stupid prank. We didn't need to go to the doughnut shop. We could all be home by now." She stopped to breathe.

"It is not your fault." That sounded so lame; obviously it was not her fault. "Natasha decided to give me a ride, not you." That came out so wrong.

"Oh what, so you're blaming Natasha now?" Elke screamed at me. "It's me, it's always me. I make people do things. I make it seem like it's all fun and no one will get hurt. We drove into a fucking wildfire.

Do you think Natasha would have done that on her own? Would you have? No. And Darius is the same. Wanting to prove he could help save us all. And look where it got him." She gulped in more air. "It's me. I'm reckless, like my father. That's what my mom says. I don't know when things have gone too far, always egging everyone to take it that bit farther. Testing people's limits."

"But you didn't. This was not your fault!"

Elke carried on like she hadn't heard a word I'd said. "We won't make it out of here, and she'll never even know where I was." She slumped to the ground, face contorted with grief and pain. "It will be just like when Dad died. She won't even get to say goodbye."

I hugged her. I didn't know what else to do. She sobbed in my arms.

The roar of the fire was getting closer. "We need to get out of here. Like now!"

Sparks spun in the smoke, fell on the ground, and skipped along the road.

She shook her head. "What's the point? We can't outrun it." She looked so forlorn, hope dying in her eyes.

"There are no bodies, so we don't know if they're even hurt, let alone dead. They might need us. They might be looking for us right now, or they might have gotten a ride and be waiting for us at the evacuation center. I don't know. But that's the point, we don't know. Let's not give up until we run out of every option."

Elke looked at me like I was spouting nonsense.

"I mean it. You have to hope for the best." Even when you knew it was pointless. It didn't matter if it was them or not. Someone had crashed here and probably hurt themselves badly. They may have died. My heart caught. Nope, I could not go there. "Elke, we've got to go."

She looked down at her boots. Her chin trembled and her shoulders shook.

"Elke, *please,* just imagine how Darius and Natasha will feel if they find out you gave up? And all the pain you're feeling right now will be how they feel when they find out you didn't make it. Come on. We can do this." *Shit, shit, come on, Elke.* I shook her arm. "Come on, we're getting out of here. Would you rather die here because you gave up, or die trying to make it out?"

She just stared at me.

"That's it. I'm not dying for you." I walked off and left her. I left her! I dare not turn around. *Please run after me. Please run after me.*

I heard her shuffle and moan and then finally the thump of her footsteps as she raced to catch up. "Were you really going to leave me?" she stuttered in disbelief.

I shook my head. "Of course not. But I wasn't going to let you give up either."

She nodded and wiped her tears away with her palms. "It's just so hard."

"I know. I've got you. You don't have to be the brave one all the time."

Swirls of ash blew into our faces. The fire roared and crackled, like waves crashing onto the shore. We ran like we were racing the wind.

33

THERE WAS A LARGE SIGN AHEAD PROCLAIMING MISSION
Middle School, Home of the Ravens. It looked more like a prison
than a school, with a high chain-link fence all the way around and
tired, dusty-looking shrubs in front of that. The main building was
large and concrete, with a small parking lot and a row of distressed-
looking conifer trees alongside, distorted by the whipping wind.
Temporary classroom trailers and a smaller box of a building with
no windows at all stood to the side of the main building.

An ambulance's spinning lights were just visible, reflecting off the
concrete walls of the smaller building. If we could just reach it quickly
enough, we'd get help and maybe a ride out of here.

"Quick, come on, come on," I urged Elke, pulling her along by
her arm. She was still in a blurred state of stupor, torn between
wanting to survive and the hopelessness of it all. I had to guide her
out of it.

I could just hear what must have been an EMT shouting instruc-
tions. "We are going to get you out of here as fast as possible."

"Almost there," I said, practically dragging Elke. "Come on, we don't want to miss this!" Where was the stupid side entrance? The fence seemed never-ending.

The EMT yelled out again, "The quicker we do this, the quicker we get you out and come back for any others!"

"There! There, people!" I pointed at the small crowd, gathered around the back of the ambulance. They were tired, sweaty, and smoke-stained. Could they even see us?

"You go, I'll wait for the next one." Elke sniffed forlornly.

"There might not be a next one." I shoved her forward. She tripped over her own feet. It was like herding a toddler.

The cluster of people rushed the ambulance doors, pushing and shoving as they tried desperately to climb onboard. A mother and child were separated. The child screamed until they were reunited. The siren's wail faded in and out with the wind. Children cried, and an old woman pounded the ambulance door with her walking stick, demanding to be let on. Two more people appeared from the back of the school, running, collapsing, and dragging themselves on. There was no way that many people could fit onboard.

"Let's go, let's go. Hurry. Hurry," the EMT yelled as she helped the two newcomers in.

"Hey! Hey!" I shouted. If she could just see us, she'd wait for us. She had to. "Come on! Come on! Climb the fence." I pushed my way through the shrubbery, pulling Elke with me.

The ambulance doors slammed shut. That sound jolted my heart. No, I was not giving up. I scrambled up the fence. If I could make it, I could get them to wait for Elke. She'd barely got her foot on the fence. The ambulance engine purred. *Shit.*

I swayed from the top of the fence, one foot each side, and tried to scream out, "Wait for us!" But my throat was so dry it came out like a pleading whisper.

The EMT didn't even see us. Nobody knew we were here.

I looked over at Elke. I could tell from her clenched jaw that she totally got the situation as well.

"We were so close," I said as the ambulance disappeared from view.

I dodged as a spark flew past my ear. The wind blasted the trees, sending smoke from side to side. Spot fires were flaring up everywhere. Too many, too fast to stamp out. My heart raced. I needed to run. But there was nowhere to run to.

Elke and I exchanged incredulous looks. It was a disaster unfurling in real time. Fire roared along the roadside, blazing with ferocious, unstoppable, annihilating heat.

"You think they'll come back?" Elke whispered.

I shrugged. "I don't know, but I'm not waiting around for them." I looked wildly around us. Buildings that could catch fire super-fast, towering trees, rushing fire. *Shit, shit, shit.* "Come on." I had no idea what I was doing but running away from the fire seemed like a smart choice. "Keep climbing. If the ambulance comes back, it will come back here." It definitely seemed like some kind of pickup point.

We dropped to the other side of the fence and ran toward the buildings. Something about being close to the wall made me feel safer. As if I could hide from the fire in the shadows.

"Plan A, the ambulance comes back and takes us," I said with a grimace to Elke. "Plan B we…" My voice faded out. What was plan

B? "We lie under these foil blankets on the blacktop?" At least it was concrete. Maybe the fire would go around us. Yeah, and maybe not. Realistically, there was no way I was lying down for the fire. I just couldn't. There had to be another way.

"Do you really think Natasha and Darius made it?" Her mind was still on that burned-out bike.

"Yes, of course." It didn't really matter. If we didn't make it, we'd never know anyway. "There's no way they didn't make it."

Focus, focus. How were we going it make it? Break into the school or lying flat on the parking lot? Trees were exploding along the road. I was not going to go out like this. The school had to offer better shelter than being outside.

I stared up at the sign, Block A. So many windows, so many doors. "Come on!" I ran behind the building in search of a wing with few windows. "Come *on!*" I yelled.

Elke spun around. I thought she was looking for an escape, but no. "Darius promised to come back for us. If he's still…" She swallowed, not daring to go there.

"He'll come back for us if he can," I said. "So, we better stay alive, right?" I coughed and felt my lungs virtually collapse under the weight of ash I'd inhaled.

The fire was so close. Why would anyone come back and risk their lives just in case there were a few stragglers left behind? They probably couldn't even get back.

"Find a section that's not all windows. We need to break in," I ordered. Why were there so many windows? We couldn't run for it, not with the smoke this thick. We wouldn't last two minutes.

"Break in how?" Elke coughed. "It's not going to help."

"We've got to try!" I ran over to a door marked Multipurpose Room. It was wooden, and maybe I could break it down. "Here, Elke, here!"

Far off, a siren wailed. No way was it going to reach us in time if it was even coming for us.

I looked up at the tiny windows, set in concrete. Great, all we needed to do was break down the door. I kicked it hard. Elke stood still, staring at the flames.

The fire raced up the road, exploding pine needles and setting all the trees blazing like giant torches. They withered in moments to shards of black gnarled limbs. Waves of fiery orange shimmered through the scattering of homes past the school, shattering windows, burning white hot and bright as a furnace, leaving nothing but black, twisted metal and ashy bones in its wake. A row of houses burned to the foundations, becoming a home graveyard in minutes.

I kicked at the wooden door, again and again. It was our only chance. "Elke!" I shouted at her. "Help!"

She shook her head, like she was coming to her senses and copied me. Her boots pounded against the door. There was a tiny crack and that was it.

"Keep trying." I coughed and kicked, and coughed and cried, and carried on kicking. I'd kick until the fire came. It was so hot. Sparks whirled above our heads. "Shit, shit, shit."

We kicked harder.

"It's not going to work!" Elke stopped. She was right. "We tried." Elke squeezed my hand, which sent a lovely warm shimmer through me. "Friends till the end." She smiled.

"We are?" I asked, trying so hard not to cry. I could feel the heat on my skin, and I knew for sure Elke could, too.

"Of course," And she hugged me. "Frenemies to besties."

"I was always jealous of you. What a waste," I said. "When all this time, we could have been such good friends."

"I know, but now we are. And I love it." And she gave a sad smile. I clutched Elke's hand. "Friends to the bitter end."

Her fingers interlaced with mine. Tears trembled at the corners of her eyes. Please don't tell me we'll be fine. I couldn't handle it. I couldn't handle any of it.

I felt dizzy and light-headed. "You should call your mom," I said.

"Yes, and you should call yours."

And say what? Goodbye? It was too much. Ash fell softly as snow—gentle, gray, poisonous snow. We were trapped.

34

"HELLO, HELLO?" A VOICE ECHOED FAINTLY AROUND THE brick walls.

I shouted back, "Hello!" Were we actually being rescued?

Two middle-aged hikers staggered around the corner of Block A. I guess they missed the evacuation, too. Their brown faces were ashen and their eyes red-rimmed. They held each other's arms tightly, as if they couldn't walk alone. They'd lost one of the hiking sticks and their backpacks.

"We missed the evacuation," the woman said, wheezing in between every word. "We heard you." She swallowed.

"We thought you might have a plan," added the guy, with a deep, husky voice.

"We kind of do," I said and pointed at the door. "Hey, can I use your stick?"

He frowned but passed it to me.

"Elke, quick!"

"Oh my God!" the woman screamed. "It's coming! *It's coming!*"

The sky turned extinction black. Ash rained down on our heads.

Fire flared up on the trees, turning them to gnarled branches in seconds. It sent sparks like fireworks ahead that caught hold of everything in their path—running along fences, buildings, vehicles, and on to the middle school buildings. A ball of fire fell onto one of the temporary classrooms, melting the paint work before dying. Everything around us was burning to ash.

We had this one chance.

"Elke." I pointed to the dumpster by the wall. We both scrambled up. I could almost reach the tiny window. Elke boosted me even higher so I could smash it with the hiking stick. I barely cracked it and almost lost my balance.

The heat seared my skin, my lungs, my brain.

"I gotcha," said Elke, pushing me even higher. Like the flames weren't almost on us. Like our lives didn't depend on it—on me.

I took a deep breath and struck again at the window. It finally cracked apart, shards smashing to the floor inside. I scrambled my boots up the wall and made a desperate attempt to haul myself up to the window. For a second, I was stuck, trapped by the narrow frame. I smashed the rest of the glass shards out of the way with my fist wrapped tightly in my hoodie sleeve and wiggled through.

I dropped down onto a huge stack of chairs that cascaded as they broke my fall. Then I was up and running, racing for the door. I unlocked it and swung it open for Elke and the two hikers to pile in. I gave them my foil blanket. Elke and I could shelter under hers.

Double protection in case the building didn't hold. "We should probably stay in the center in case any or the walls catch fire." I couldn't believe I was saying this. As if there was any hope we wouldn't be burned alive in there.

"Bless you. Thank you," The couple hugged me, then held hands, crying and praying. Whatever happened, at least they had each other.

Elke and I huddled together on the hard, shiny floor, under the silver foil blanket, like some kind of hellish campout. Waiting for the worst. I checked my phone. Surprise, no signal. It would have been overloaded by emergency calls, even if there was one. I wrote Mom a text anyway.

Love you mom. I tried.

I deleted *I tried* in case I made it.

Elke tapped out something on hers and gave me a sad grin. "She deserves to know. I do love her, you know."

"I know." I sighed. No more hiding. I had to get it out. "About that night, back at Yosemite camp." My chin quivered. "I honestly didn't remember. I kicked the ember and you saw me! Why didn't you say anything?"

"It looked like an impulse, just curiosity. Misguided, but not worth ruining a life over. And no one got hurt. You shouted 'Fire' as soon as you realized."

"Is that supposed to make me feel better? I don't know why I did it." Why twelve-year-old Lily did it. I couldn't hide from her anymore. "I hadn't meant to hurt anyone. I was so screwed up by everything, Natasha, Mom, and you." I stopped talking. I could hardly breathe. Tears ran down my cheeks. "Thank you for knowing and not hating me."

Elke squeezed my hand. "Everyone makes mistakes. The trick is to learn from them."

"Sometimes you sound so wise."

"Only sometimes?"

I closed my eyes and listened to the world crumble outside. The sound was overwhelming, a constant rush and roar—giant blazing waves of fire. The heat, the air sucking heat, and the acrid stench of fear, and the crackle, and it was all getting louder as it came for us.

"Do you really think they made it?" Elke whispered. I knew she meant Natasha and Darius.

"Yes, for sure, they're out there riding away together." I prayed that was true.

"And they'll know we're together, and we made it, too. Because wishing for a happy ending has to work this time. *It has to.*" Elke could hardly speak from holding in all her sadness.

I could see little cracks of pain opening back up, and all I could do was hold her tight, tell her that we were going to be okay, everything was going to be fine, and we'd be listening to her road trip CD in no time. If only I believed that myself.

I could hear the hiker couple praying together, mumbling in low earnest voices.

"Please don't let me die. Please don't let me die." I'd never see Mom again.

Elke gripped my hand. "We die or survive, together," she pledged.

Frenemies become best friends in the face of death—the perfect headline. A sob rose in my chest.

I shut my eyes against the scorching heat that moved in waves around us. The heat sucked everything out of the air. Too intense to breathe or think. We just lay there praying, not even hoping, just please let me live, please let me live. Please let me die of smoke inhalation, not fire.

Elke's hot breath blew against my ear. "If we burn to death, we'll be fused together," she rasped. I found that weirdly comforting.

Our tears merged into a river trailing down our stained faces.

"I believe in you more than anyone in the world. And your hair smells of Barbie dolls and summer." I just wanted her to know that.

"I believe in you, too," she murmured. "Do you think he's waiting for me?"

"Your dad?"

She nodded.

"No, he's rooting for you." I squeezed her so tightly there was no space between us. Her heart beat with mine, racing to destiny. "He knows you're going to make it."

"And if we don't?" she asked.

And the ash, the flames, and the voices stilled. For a second everything was silent, a void of blank emptiness.

"We won't know." Pain, fear, and heartbreak for everything that could have been, Mom devastated, my small life reduced to dust in the wind.

I wasn't going to say that out loud and lend it a fighting chance of becoming reality. Like I had any control over a wildfire. "When we get out, I'm going to make my life matter and be somebody I'm proud of." Life isn't about being happy and safe; it's about dealing with the challenges, growing from them, and moving on.

Elke touched my face with her soft, sweaty hand. "In that case, we *are* going to make it," she said murmured. "We—" She waited for me to join in.

"*Are* going to make it," I whispered. Then I clasped her hand in mine and smiled through my tears. "We *are* going to make it," I said louder.

The fire was seizing hold of the school. I could hear the other windows shattering. Flames raced across the outside walls, crackling like a thousand firecrackers exploding at once, rolling and falling in a great gust of heat waves so thick, the air moved with them.

It was too hot to breathe. Too hot to move. Too hot to think.

The foil blanket quivered against my trembling skin. Sweat trickled down my shins. I could hear Elke's breath came out in little tremors. There was no air, just a searing vacuum of heat. I jolted as part of the ceiling caved in and smashed on the floor. There was a loud rumbling like a freight train racing along its tracks, coming straight for us. I cowered under the foil and clasped Elke's sweaty hand even tighter. She squeezed back and made a tiny whimper.

My lungs were on fire. I shut my eyes against the searing heat. It was too hot to see. *This was it. This was it.* The flame train raced above our heads on invisible tracks, shaking, shaking, shaking everything right down to my bones. Its roar filled every space, a rush of sound that never ended. The whole building trembled. The air rippled with heat waves.

Sections of the walls were smashing around us, shattering on impact. Concrete clattered down in what sounded like massive chunks bouncing across the floor. Explosions came from everywhere, too many, too fast. I winced at every sound. It was never going to end. The whole world was on fire, roaring and collapsing in on itself. Then suddenly the fire train rushed on through, leaving only the faint patter of ash falling like hail.

There was a hush.

35

"WE MADE IT," I WHISPERED TO ELKE.

"Yes," she whispered back.

We stood in the middle of what used to be a multipurpose room. Piles of rubble and white ash lay all around. A third of the ceiling had burned away, and the top of one of the side walls. Steel skeletons twisted where there used to be concrete, poking out like long fingernails. The remains of the ceiling were blackened with soot. The walls were smoke-stained and covered with what looked like peeling paper. The entrance door swung to and fro, creaking in the wind. The frame had survived and the concrete around it, but the corner of that wall had disappeared, as if the fire had come right up and taken a gigantic bite out of the building.

There was a display on the far wall celebrating Mission Middle School, Home of the Ravens. One panel was almost untouched, the colored-paper ravens barely even smoke-damaged. The other panel was a mess of burned paper, scorch marks, and soot. The fire damage seemed so random and unpredictable—all or almost nothing.

The air was thick with sepia haze. I tried not to breathe in the acrid smoke and ash. There was an underlying scent of burned plastic and sulfur. I was desperate to leave but couldn't move.

"Fuck," Elke murmured.

I nodded. Every part of me trembled. Even my veins felt like they were vibrating. I was so hot and so cold at the same time. I couldn't stop blinking. My eyes were too dry to cry, my throat too tight to swallow, my lungs too heavy to breathe. We'd made it. We were still here, still alive. Somehow miraculously, we'd survived.

"Ready?" Elke squeezed my hand.

"Yep." I gave her a weak smile, and we made our way over to the two hikers, who stood staring around the building in shock.

They told us their names. At least I think that's what they were saying. It was hard to hold a thought in my head, right then.

The guy shook his head. "You saved our lives. I just..." He struggled to find the words.

"You were so brave, thank you," the woman finished.

"Of course." I smiled back awkwardly. "It was instinct. I didn't know what I was doing."

They hugged us both and finally we made our way outside. Part of me wondered if there was still an outside there. As if we could walk out into a blank void of nothing. It was so quiet.

I needed to see where we would have had to lie outside if we hadn't found shelter. Where we were supposed to lie flat under a sheet of foil, and somehow survive. At the same time, I didn't want to see it. But we couldn't hide in this shell of a building forever. The ceiling had been damaged and the roof was caved in at the end. The whole place stank of smoke, burning plastic and wood. But it had to be safer outside, now the fire had passed.

Ash rained down on our faces and gathered on the parking lot like heaps of snow—if snow were made of death and despair.

"You okay?" Elke tugged on my arm. "You're trembling and bleeding!"

"I am?" I looked down at my hands, I was. "Adrenaline and glass."

"Here," she wrapped her mask tightly around my cut hand and bound it in place with her shoelace. "Hold it up above your heart. There you go. Told you we'd make it."

"Thank you." I could hardly breathe, but we *had* made it.

We hugged, then broke apart and giggled but stopped because we were still in hell. It was nine o'clock in the morning and still dark as twilight.

Embers lit up a path across the middle school rubble. The fire had left a smoldering blackness in its wake. Cars, trees, and road signs were all warped and melted, mangled as if a bomb had exploded. The plastic dumpster lid had melted. And the many-windowed class-rooms at the front were a mess of melted tables and chairs, twisted metal legs and ash. So much ash. And a thick silence, broken only by a bird singing desperately from a blackened branch.

We'd almost died. People had died, and it didn't matter who they were, they were all loved. Everything welled up inside and came crashing out. I sobbed for them all. And Elke sobbed with me. We'd been to hell and come out the other side.

A fire truck pulled up to the school. They'd come back to check if anyone left behind needed help getting to the emergency shelter. Fortunately, we were fine, so they gave us directions and went on their way searching for any other survivors. The shelter wasn't far, barely a mile farther down the road.

We started walking, stopping every now and then and staring in stunned disbelief at the scorched landscape around us. It was like a disaster movie set. Homes completely burned to the ground, reduced to ash with just the chimney and the brick fireplace standing, next to homes that were virtually untouched. But we were still here, and we were okay.

I checked my phone, which was completely drained of battery. Figures.

"You got any power?" I asked Elke, showing her my phone.

She pulled out her own. "Crap, no. I bet we can power them up at the emergency shelter."

"I bet Darius and Natasha are okay. If we made it, they must have." I was trying to convince myself more than Elke.

Elke sighed. "I hope so. If anyone can make it, it's Natasha."

"Then I'm right." Natasha might not be a close friend anymore, but in a weird way, I still loved her. Now that Elke and I were friends, I appreciated Natasha more. And that made it worse. Why did the cuts from childhood hurt the most?

There were still occasional sparks and glowing embers, nestled in the debris. Animals wandering by looking just as dazed as us, deer, quails, even a bobcat running along what was once the tree line. One leap and it was gone into what used to be the woods.

I had no idea how devastating a fire could be, about as bad as your worst nightmare, times a thousand. Flakes of ash were in our hair, our skin, our eyelashes. Tall trees were blackened and hollowed, and buildings burned to white ash. There were a few straggling people, red-eyed and dazed, looking for people whose names they couldn't remember. People they might never find.

It made my knees buckle just thinking about it, so I focused on finding Natasha instead.

Elke looked around. "You reckon they'll have anything to eat at the emergency shelter?"

"God, I hope so." I was suddenly ravenous.

A dog ran over to us from the other side of the road—a husky with big blue eyes. It barked happily and ran in circles. You'd never know it was in a disaster area and had just missed burning to death.

"Hi, Snowdrop," I said, seeing the name on her collar. I looked around at the few stragglers walking on the road, but nobody appeared to be looking for a missing dog. She wagged her tail eagerly. I looked at the address on her tag. It probably didn't exist anymore. "Let's bring her to the shelter with us."

"Of course," Elke agreed, and she bent down and scratched Snowdrop's ears.

I knew Snowdrop probably had an owner that missed her terribly. But I could pretend she was mine for a little while. I kissed her soft head and scrunched my nose when she licked me.

We walked down the road, trying not to look in the burned-out cars. "Oh God," I grabbed Elke's arm. There was a body that looked more like a skeleton in one of the cars.

"We're okay," Elke reminded me. "And Darius and Natasha will be, too."

I nodded. They had to be.

Snowdrop trotted along happily between us, as if she knew exactly where we were going. The sky was burnt gold and full of sepia smoke. Better than blazing orange, but still surreal. It had to be midmorning by now. The whole place could be anywhere, anytime. We were moving through a parallel world where everything could be lost in a second, and nothing was permanent or real. Everything mattered so much and not at all.

As I walked, I felt the pulse of my own heartbeat and had no choice but to listen to my thoughts. I was alive, what did I want? I imagined myself at Oak Canyon College, walking over the bridge between the dorms and the rest of campus. Laughing with friends in the Commons Café.

But it hit me that this future did not need to be perfect; it didn't need to be all or nothing. If Mom was sick again, we'd deal with it together. I could go to community college and transfer to Oak Canyon in a year or two. Or take a semester break, or a gap year off. Whatever happened, we'd figure it out. It would be okay.

I took a deep breath and gave Elke a quick smile. "So what's next for you?"

We crossed a road, stepping over a smoldering tire by the curb before she answered. "That year in eighth grade was the worst year of my life. I will never let anyone, or anything make me feel like that again."

Snowdrop barked, almost as if in agreement.

"That campfire night and everything after was hideous, but I was already hollow." She blinked back a tear. "Dad had that stupid bike accident, and I didn't get to say goodbye. We couldn't get back to Amsterdam in time." She paused and swallowed. "When we got there, all that was left was a watch and a broken phone that they'd put in a plastic bag for us."

"I'm so sorry." I wanted to say sorry forever. But every time I said it, the word lost a little more weight and sounded more meaningless. I looked up at the forbidding sky. "I was so caught up in my own problems, I didn't see anyone else's."

"It's called being a kid," Elke gave me a sad smile. "We've all been there. I didn't know how close you were to Natasha, or that I marched in and stomped all over your friendship."

I drew myself up. "It was only a matter of time. I just couldn't see it. Afterward when all the gossip hit, Natasha said I was a clingy loser, and she didn't care what you did, because you'd still be a million times better than me anyway."

"I bet you were pleased I'd gone," said Elke.

"Yes, and no. Like yes, because I thought I'd get Natasha back as a friend, and no because after you left, I realized I wasn't jealous of Natasha. I was jealous because I wanted you to be my friend. When you left, I cried for weeks. And me and Natasha were never close again."

"But you still took her up on a ride offer?" Elke linked my arm in hers.

I laughed. "Yes, idiot that I am. I figured water under the bridge. Anyway, it was just a ride."

I pulled Snowdrop back from the burned body of some kind of animal.

"Would you have come, if you'd known I'd be there?"

I nodded and focused on the road so Elke wouldn't see how close I was to tears. I stumbled over the curb as we continued walking downhill. "Everyone thinks I was spying on the party, and all I did was shout 'Fire' to get you in trouble. No one but you knows the truth." I blinked a tear from my eye. I didn't want to talk about this. Not when everything around us was such a disaster zone. And I was heading home to more bad news. "I would have said no, if I'd known, but I'm glad I said yes."

"I know what you mean." Elke stared straight ahead.

My heartbeat thumped in my ears. "I hope we can stay friends this time." I blurted it out and waited to fall into a black hole of rejection.

"Me too. I'm still here." Elke smiled. "And I'm not going anywhere."

36

THE EMERGENCY SHELTER TURNED OUT TO BE A VETER-
ans' memorial hall, just down the road and well out of the way of the
wildfire's path. Inside was a long table full of granola bars, water bottles,
and Gatorade, and white N95 masks. Rows and rows of low beds were
lined up across the hall, mostly claimed by sprawled families.

We each grabbed a water bottle. Kids raced between the beds,
playing like nothing unusual had happened. It was a relief to see
something normal and sweet.

I led Snowdrop to a water fountain and filled a paper bowl for her
to drink from. "Any word on who got out?" I asked a guy ambling
past.

Nearby was a notice board that was starting to fill with Post-it
Notes for people looking for missing loved ones.

"I'll ask around about Natasha and Darius," said Elke and disappeared into the back of the shelter.

"I don't know, Snowdrop. We'd better make a sign for you." I
kissed her head, and she looked up at me with her ice-blue husky
eyes. I took a Post-it and wrote,

FOUND SNOWDROP—HUSKY DOG, and left my phone number.

She was so sweet, but I couldn't take her just because I needed a friend. I would only keep her with me until I got her somewhere safe.

Safe. Shit, I needed to check on Mom.

I pulled out my phone, forgetting the battery was dead. But I wasn't sure I was ready to go back into the real world yet, for the bombardment of texts that would appear and the bad news. For a moment, I just needed to be.

Elke came back over, waving her phone. "No one's seen them. And no message from Natasha."

"It's okay, she's going to be okay. She's Natasha." Please let her be okay.

"Maybe." Elke smiled sadly. "She'd have gotten someone to help her out of whatever tight situation she got in. Probably Darius."

I had a sinking feeling we were taking turns trying to convince each other she and Darius were fine. But why wouldn't they be here? "Let's just keep asking around. Someone must have seen them."

A friendly lady with silver bobbed hair and a padded jacket lent me her charger. I plugged my phone into an outlet near her chair and left it with her while I continued to search for answers. New people were arriving with that ashen, shaken, stunned look. I wondered if we looked like that, too.

Snowdrop looked up at me like she was waiting for something. I figured she was hungry and took a granola bar for me, and a beef stick for her from the snack table. I gulped it in three bites. Snowdrop ate hers in one.

"Good job. You were meant to be her rescuer," said Elke.

"I think she needs to go out." She'd been pulling that way, so I figured she needed a pee.

We put on the N95 masks and went out to the parking lot. It was still smoky, but a million times better than before.

"Hey!" a voice called out.

We turned and recognized the truck and the guys who'd picked us up, Ryan and Chase, leaning against it.

Elke gasped. "Oh my God, you made it and your truck too!"

"Yep! We had to go back for that," said Ryan. "Super lucky it wasn't in the fire's path."

Chase grinned like we were old friends. "That was brave what you two did, leaving the truck and making a run for it. We were too scared to move."

"Until I persuaded him it was our best chance." Ryan smiled at me. "Thank God, you're here. We were so worried after you ran off. We ditched the truck and ran across the bridge, and this amazing firefighter broke into a Walgreens and saved our lives."

"You got saved by Walgreens?" I laughed.

Ryan beamed and put his hand on his heart. "Now we've been through this together, we're family. Anything you need, just ask."

"A ride then?" Elke asked. "Someone at the emergency shelter said people are gathering at the freeway exit, at Rice Hill Inn, to get rides and check in on official missing people updates."

"Sounds like a good plan," Chase nodded. "Whenever you're ready."

"Oh shit, my phone." I ran inside and thanked the kind woman who'd lent me her charger and turned to go.

"You've got a call," she yelled after me. My stomach flipped. It would be Mom. I couldn't handle that yet. I thanked her, slipped the phone into my pocket, and ran back out.

They dropped us off at the inn, with promises to call them when we got home, to stay in touch, look after ourselves, and not get caught in any other wildfires. It was like they were our surrogate uncles.

The Rice Hill Inn was a motel with an attached diner. It was heaving with people, having become a kind of drop-off point for anyone looking for a ride out of there. Everyone was disheveled, drinking coffee, corralling children, and talking urgently on phones.

I finally checked my phone. Yes, Mom had called. It was time to face reality.

"Mom?" Just saying her name made me choke up.

"Lily? Oh my God. Thank God, you're okay. Oh, honey," and I could hear her burst into tears.

It was a long and complicated call as I tried to explain everything that had happened. Well, not everything. Not the encounter with Neil, or that we'd split up with Natasha who might have broken her ankle and was now missing, or that we'd almost died. Just the "we are okay" basics. But I did ask her about her test. Snowdrop stayed at my side the whole time.

It was hard to end the call, like neither one of us wanted to hang up. "Love you too, Mom," I told her. "See you soon. I promise we'll come straight home. Goodbye, bye, bye." Why did I say that? I had no idea how we were going to get home. But I knew we would. We had to.

I put my phone down and looked up at Elke.

"She's"—I didn't know how to start—"not clear, but the tumors are shrinking." I collapsed against the wall. "She's not dying. All that time I thought she was dying." I covered my mouth with my hand, which didn't help as my whole face collapsed.

Elke hugged me. "That's such good news."

I nodded. "It is." It meant so much. Mom wanted me to live my dreams, but I wanted her to be okay. "Oh, did you speak to your mom?"

Elke smiled. "She hopped on a flight from Oakland to Portland as soon as she heard about the wildfires and couldn't get ahold of me. We did all that driving, and it's only just over an hour flight! She picked up a rental car at Portland airport and she's on her way here now. Lucky we moved back to San Ramon this summer, so we can drop you off, no problem!" Her face suddenly fell. "But no one's heard from Darius or Natasha."

I squeezed her hand. "We'll find them."

"Hey, hey, enough of that!"

We spun around.

Natasha hobbled toward us, with Darius right behind her. "Oh, my God, you're alive!" And she smashed herself right into us both.

Darius grinned like he was at a loss for words, while the three of us just collapsed in each other's arms.

"We skidded on the motorcycle. The roads were full of abandoned cars, and downed trees, chunks of burning bark," Natasha finally explained. "We left it, ran, and got a ride from a passing ambulance."

"It was totally squashed full of people. But they got us out of there and dropped us off at urgent care. And then we came to wait for you here. I knew you'd make it. And there was no way Natasha was leaving until you did." Darius beamed. "God, I'm so happy to see you!"

"Lily saved us!" said Elke. "Me and these two hikers. We totally wouldn't have made it without her!"

I actually blushed. "It was nothing. Anyone would have thought of it."

It had been the adrenaline and the fear, and the not wanting to die. But I couldn't help feeling a little rush of pride. Thank God it worked. The alternative was unthinkable.

Natasha beamed. "I knew you'd be okay together! All I got was a new nickname. See," she held out her foot, now wearing a giant black boot. "I'm now officially Big Foot!"

We all laughed. It was such a relief, and so surreal to be back together, changed and not changed.

I was so happy to see Natasha again. It was like none of our past differences mattered. "I'm sorry for everything." I know, I've said it a million times, but something felt like this would be the last. "Not just for Yosemite camp, but for everything."

"I know, me too." Natasha hugged me. It was all over. Finally, we could move on. "Do you both have a ride home? We can take you." She laughed. "I understand if you'd rather not."

"A friend of mine is coming for us," Darius explained. "He's waiting outside."

"We're good," said Elke. "My mom's coming."

We waited with Darius and Natasha until their ride pulled up. Then we all hugged and promised to stay in touch. Maybe Natasha and I would say more than hi in the hallway at school now.

She looked so happy, waving from the back seat of the car, a bright-purple Tesla.

"At least we won't lose sight of them," Elke joked as we waved them off.

We stood outside the Rice Hill Inn, watching the Tesla take the freeway entrance by the inn. The bright car smoothly joined the slow-moving traffic that wound up the hill and disappeared into the smoky haze.

"I'm so glad Natasha is giving Darius another chance. They both look so happy." I grinned at Elke. "At least it's not so far to Davis."

"Yep, only nine hours to go!" Elke smiled. "Okay, let's go find my mom."

My phone buzzed with a voicemail message.

"Something wrong?" Elke asked, as I listened to it.

The message was from a woman who said she was a volunteer at the emergency shelter where I'd posted my note about Snowdrop. I braced myself, but the news wasn't what I thought it would be. I listened to it twice in case I'd gotten it wrong. Then blinked back happy tears.

I hung up the phone and told Elke. "They found Snowdrop's owner. He's lost his house and has to go into a senior living facility. He wonders if I'd be willing to keep Snowdrop forever. For *real*. He wants her to go to a good home." Tears welled up again, and I wondered if this was my life now, where all my emotions were on the edge of tipping over all the time.

"Will your mom mind if I bring a dog?" I sniffled.

"Some road trip, hey?" Elke's mom asked.

Elke and I rested against each other in the backseat of her mom's rented RAV4. Snowdrop lay at our feet, fast asleep. We both smiled and nodded, too tired to talk.

"Never going to leave California again," I murmured to Elke.

"I don't blame you," Elke said. "But now that your mom's doing better, you can think more about college, right?"

"Yes." I felt a buzz of hope. "I know where I want to be, if they'll have me."

"Why wouldn't they?" Elke grinned. "You're a great catch." She squeezed my hand. "I've been thinking, I'm not ready for college yet, at least not full time, but maybe a community college or a part-time thing could work. I don't know. But if you and Natasha are all about leaving home and adulting, perhaps I should be, too. At least we live in the same town again." She nudged me and smiled. "I hope you know what you're getting into, now that we're friends. I'll be bugging you for game nights, movie marathons, maybe some dog walking." She stroked Snowdrop's ears. "I might even bring another friend along. You used to be pretty close."

"Sounds perfect," I said. And could not stop smiling the whole way home.

One Year Later

AFTERNOON

Friday, August 23

37

TEN HOURS IN THE CAR WAS A LONG TIME BUT SO FAR there had been no fires, no delays, and no detours—unless you include stopping off for a fancy lunch. I guess that's what happens when you have your mom drive.

Snowdrop leaned into me. "Hey, you good, sweet doggo. We're almost at our new home!"

She put her paw on my hand and looked up at me with those big blue husky eyes. I kissed her all over her face. I was so glad she was coming, too.

I glanced at Mom as she sang off-key to the radio. She was trying so hard to be happy. But she stopped singing as we pulled past the Oak Canyon College sign and into the next oak-tree-lined road on the right.

"Wow, even the air smells better. Perhaps I should move up here. It's got to be cheaper than San Ramon. I could get a nice little crafts-man house. You could move in with me. They'd be room for your roommate." She grinned as I shook my head.

We both knew she was joking, but also not. She so wanted this for me.. And if anything happened, if her treatment stopped working, we'd figure it out. I wasn't her only support system anymore. She assured me she'd be fine. Alone doesn't mean lonely, she kept reminding me. It was time for her to be free and live her life, too. Starting with a tour of Scotland with my Scottish gran to find their roots.

Which left me to finally live my life, guilt-free.

My stomach was a hive of bees as I jumped out the car and ran up to the bronze-clad walls of the apartment block, my new home. It glinted with promise. A three-story building with a balcony and a view of downtown Portland. Oak Canyon College was just a short walk away.

My heart pounded. This was it, the beginning of everything. No, not the beginning, the next chapter. All the mistakes, the experiences, the friendships lost and found, had led up to this.

I let out my breath slowly. So funny to think Natasha was doing the same thing in a different place. Not Stanford, but UC Davis. I grinned to myself. She'd promised to come up and visit. I assumed she'd fly, not drive.

Mom tapped me on the shoulder. "Are you really ready for this?"

I nodded. I knew she had tears in her eyes, just like I did. Bittersweet, a new start for both of us.

"I am so proud of you, Lily. I want you to be so happy, honey." Mom smiled at me and wiped her eyes. "I hope you love your roommate."

"Oh, I know I will!" I beamed. I was happy, and sad, and hopeful, and petrified, and so very alive. My skin tingled with the everything of it all.

And then Elke came flying out of the entrance, running like she was on fire, and hugged me like she'd never let me go.

ACKNOWLEDGMENTS

THE SPARK FOR THIS STORY CAME FROM REGULAR ROAD trips up and down the mountainous I-5 route from the San Francisco Bay Area, up to Portland and back again. And yes, it takes ten hours on a good day—with only a quick gas and coffee refill break!

These trips started just as the West Coast wildfire season seemed to really heat up. Every year there were unprecedented fires that sent firestorms across the landscape, razed towns, and turned the sky bright orange. The mountains became almost invisible in the hazy smoke-filled air, and detours and road closures became common. It was surreal and terrifying. Suddenly it was here—in our hometown, the air thick with smoke, our bags packed and ready to go, as we listened for the evacuation warnings.

Fortunately, the fires near us were contained, but others were not so lucky. This story is for all the firefighters, the emergency services workers, the brave souls who survived these catastrophes, and those who did not. You are all my heroes.

It takes a village to bring a story to life! So first, a huge thank-you to my awesome agent, Tara Gonzalez, who loved this idea from its tiny spark of a start. Thank you so much for always believing in my half-formed ideas and championing them all the way! You are the best!

Wendy McClure, my amazing editor, thank you so much for believing in me and this story, for your incredible guidance, insightful editorial notes, Zoom chats, and for being such a joy to work with!

Huge thanks to the Sourcebooks Fire and Sourcebooks teams for your wonderful support. To the editorial department, Jenny Lopez, editorial support, and Diane Dannenfeldt, my copy editor and proofreader—one day I will write fluently in American English! And to Thea Voutiritsas and Jessica Thelander in production; Karen Masnica, Rebecca Atkinson, and Michelle Lecumberry in marketing and publicity; and Erin Fitzsimmons, art director, for the wonderful art direction and design teams, and for the amazing cover design. And to all the brilliant people who've worked on this book, and whose names I am yet to know—I so appreciate you all!

My brilliant critique partners and besties, Lisa Ramée and Lou Minns: What would I do without your amazing support, friendship, writerly guidance, and lovely long author chats?

First readers Maya Prasad, and Vanessa Torres: Thank you so much for your caring advice and expertise. Any mistakes are mine and mine alone!

Amy Warwick, for sharing your harrowing experiences, your writing support, and so many good times and drinks at the Richmond Bar! Also, thank you, Division Inns, for being our perfect halfway meeting spot and home away from home in Portland!

Thank you so much, Kristy Boyce. Your support and friendship, means everything to me! Cindy Derby and Meg Fleming, for your amazing friendship, hugs, texts, constant love, and support! And Deborah Underwood, for always being there when I need you!

Laura Lentz and Arturo Montes, thanks for jumping in at a moment's notice with the exact info I needed! And to Pam Turner for your Oregon winery insider knowledge, your friendship, and your support.

My lovely cousin Darius and his sweet daughter Elke—thank you for your brilliant names! The characters in this story are fictional and not based on either of you, at all, except for all the nice parts!

Big thanks to my online Discord crews, you know who you are! Also #TeamTara, @22debuts and #YAKnow—for all the comradely, love, and support! Thank you, Marti Parham, for keeping our goals on track!

Special shout-out to the incredibly supportive and talented Bay Area kidlit community, especially Misa Sugiura, Stacy Lee, Randy Ribay, and Joanna Ho. Thank you for your wonderful friendship and support.

To my parents, for instilling in me a love of travel and taking me on all those road trips, where a hundred miles to go meant we were almost there!

Big thanks to my local indie Towne Center Books, for all the love. Judy, you and your team rock! To all the booksellers, book bloggers, and librarians everywhere, thank you so much for fighting the good fight and getting books into the hands of readers who need them and love them! To my readers, your support makes my heart sing!

And finally, so much love and thanks to Adam and Luka, for your constant love and for always believing in me, no matter which paths I wander! I can't think of two people I'd rather spend this road trip called life with!

ABOUT THE AUTHOR

Photo © Adam Morgan

KEELY PARRACK WAS BORN and raised in England. She is a YA and picture book author whose titles include *Don't Let in the Cold*. Keely came to America for fun twenty years ago. She is still here doing the things she loves: writing YA novels, poetry, and picture books, and motivating kids to be excited about reading and creative writing. She has worked in retail, education, and as a social networker for her local indie bookstore. When she's not brainstorming her next book, she loves to read, binge-watch horror movies, hike, travel, and take too many photographs. She lives in the San Francisco Bay Area, with her husband and son, her favorite road trip companions!

sourcebooks fire

Home of the hottest trends in YA!

Visit us online and
sign up for our newsletter at
FIREreads.com

....

Follow
@sourcebooksfire
online